Myths & Legends of TEA

Volume 1

Myths &

Legends

of

TEA

Volume 1

Gary D. Robson

Proseyr Publishing
Red Lodge, MT U.S.A.

Myths & Legends of Tea, Volume 1
By Gary D. Robson

Body copy set in Baskerville
Headings set in Avenir Light

Cover photo, "Sunset in tea plantation valley," by Nicholas Han

First edition
ISBN 978-0-9659609-5-3
9 8 7 6 5 4 3 2

Proseyr Publishing
PO Box 1630, Red Lodge, MT 59068
www.proseyr.com

*For everyone in the tea
blogging community that
has humored me, educated
me, and listened to my
stories.*

Contents

One of the most-recited myths in the tea world is that of Shennong, the legendary Chinese emperor who introduced agriculture to China, worked extensively with herbs to create the first Chinese pharmacopoeia, and invented acupuncture. In working with herbs, Shennong discovered that boiling water somehow made even "bad" water healthy to drink. One day, Shennong settles under a tree to relax with a cup of hot water. As he waits for the water to cool, leaves from the tree blow into his cup. A few minutes later, he notices a heavenly aroma rising from his cup. He raises it to his lips and becomes the first man to enjoy what is now the world's most popular drink.

Foreword

By Geoffrey Norman

I've never written a forward before. Hell, I don't think I've even *read* a forward. I usually skip that part and dive right into the introduction. What is the importance of a forward, anyway? A nod from somebody really important confirming the importance of the text succeeding it? In that case, I hate to disappoint you, fair reader, but I'm not really that important. And I have no clue what I'm doing, but I can say a few nice things about the author.

For one, the dude looks great in a kilt. What? Too forward?

Oh, quit being so damn picky! Perhaps I should tell a story, will that suffice? No, it's not long. I swear.

I first encountered Gary Robson via Twitter. He really stuck out. People wearing large hats often do. And in his mug shot, Gary was sporting a very large hat. A cowboy hat, no less. Nothing about the man screamed, "TEA!" However, I will admit, I was curious.

After some cursory social media stalking, I learned that he had my dream job – running a bookstore/tea bar. On the side, he wrote children's books about animal poop. **Dream. Job.**

The thing that intrigued me the most was that he created his own tea blends. I don't usually go for blends, but I am a sucker for a blend with a story behind it. *All* of his shop's custom blends had a story to tell. The one that grabbed my mind's eye the most was dubbed "Mr. Excellent's Post-Apocalyptic Earl Grey." Best. Tea name. Ever. And the origin story was just as epic.

I had to try it, I had to write about it, and I did both. The blend even inspired a short story that I still have … yet to write. Point being, the man knew how to spin a yarn about tea. What neither he nor any other tea author had accomplished yet, though, was chronicling the tales of tea's past.

Tea is an ancient beverage. Most of its origin stories are shrouded in myth and legend. Some teas have several origin stories, while others have no stories at all. They just appeared as if they'd always been there, all freaky-like (I'm looking at you, goeshicha).

Other teas had origins that may have had a basis in fact, but over the centuries, their stories were embellished. Can't make a white tea sound interesting? Throw a moon goddess or a dragon in there! Go nuts! What's that? A black tea that seems ordinary? Throw an emperor's mother into the mix! Eh, an oolong you can't grade accurately? Say it was picked by monkeys!

And the problem (if it can even be called that) only got worse once the Europeans got a hold of the stuff. There are no less than *five* origin stories for Earl Grey. Some hoity-toity store in London even claims to hold the "original recipe" for it. Teabags? Those, too, are often the subject of wondrous debate.

The list goes on, but no one has bothered to try and compile these wayward stories in one place. Which brings me back to the dude in a kilt-'n-cowboy hat; who better to spin a yarn or dozen about teas-that-were?

So, read on. There might even be swords.

Acknowledgements

There are some people I need to thank for their help in making this book happen, starting with my ever-patient wife, Kathy. She has listened to my stories, pushed me when I fell behind, and even taken the time to proofread this book. Our son, Doug, when he was managing our tea bar, heard these stories far too many times, and yet continued to be supportive and encouraging.

I also owe a huge thank you to the customers at the tea bar. Only by telling my stories out loud can I gauge when they're any good. You've all asked the questions that made me dig deeper for facts. You've laughed at the right times, and gazed wide-eyed when the story grows tense.

This book could not have happened without the education I've received at the hands of my friends in the tea business. Growers, importers, and distributors have all been free with their knowledge and eager to teach me about their tea. Other tea shop owners have treated me as a compatriot rather than a competitor.

And then there are the tea bloggers. I shudder when I look back at what I was writing when I started that blog in 2011, but the other bloggers didn't take me to task for it. They responded and helped me out. When I started meeting them face-to-face, I found a group of kindred spirits. That's why I dedicated this book to them.

Introduction

My love for the myths and legends of tea began when insatiable curiosity met a collection of intriguing and evocative tea names. Iron Goddess of Mercy? Who would name a tea that? Who was this Earl Grey guy, and how did he pull off all the product placements in *Star Trek: the Next Generation*?

As I learned more and more of the stories, I began to tell them to innocent patrons in my tea bar. Like any good storyteller, I started to embellish them, making them my own. People would come in just for the stories, and one day, someone asked me the obvious question:

"Why don't you write these down, Gary?"

At first, I wrote them exactly as I told them, but I came to realize that I had the opportunity to do a lot more. I want each of the stories in this book to be an insight into another culture and a glimpse at another era of history. The stories span centuries and span the globe, and this is only the first volume.

With so many stories to tell, it was difficult to decide which ones would go in volume one of *Myths & Legends*. I decided to go for variety. Not counting the prologue, this book has stories from the 16th, 18th, 19th, 20th, and 21st centuries. The stories cover Japan, China, England, Taiwan, Australia, and the United States. They tell stories of green tea, oolong tea, and black tea. The cast of characters ranges from emperors and goddesses to poor tea farmers.

Are these stories all true? Well, sort of – except for the one about the zombie apocalypse in Australia 20 years from now. That's most certainly not true. As for the others, it's complicated.

I've researched each of these myths. Some of them have been told in substantially the same way for hundreds of years. Some are told differently by every storyteller. Some are so close to reality that you could find them in a history book. And then there's that zombie one.

When I mention someone prominent, like Emperor Shennong, Tea Master Sen no Rikyū, Earl Grey, that person is mostly likely real. I have researched the settings carefully, so if these things actually happened, they probably happened very close to the time and place that I said they did.

But I used the words "myths and legends" in the title of this book for a reason. It is unlikely that a goddess actually gave a poor farmer a tea plant. Iced tea may have been "invented" independently by dozens of people before it became widespread. These are stories, and I have created characters, dialog, and events for them.

Since this is a book of myths and legends rather than a history book, I have taken liberties and done my best to make the stories entertaining and educational. I hope you enjoy them in that spirit.

Spelling the names of teas

Spelling is important to a writer, but spelling things "right" is often a difficult task when transliterating from languages that don't use our alphabet. Last year, I decided to standardize on a spelling for tieguanyin, a tea which is the subject of one of the stories in this book. In my first day at that year's World Tea Expo, I saw tieguanyin spelled at least six different ways. In fact, a quick scan of my blog showed that I had spelled it at least three different ways myself.

Tieguanyin, Tie Guanyin, Tae Guan Yin, Ti Kuan Yin, Tie Gwan Yin, Tie Kwun Yin… which one is right?

In reality, none of them are "right." The name of the tea is Chinese, which is written in Chinese characters. Even in Chinese, there are two different ways to write it (鐵觀音 in traditional Chinese and 铁观音 in simplified Chinese). Some of the sounds in Chinese don't translate clearly and unambiguously into English, and translations vary over time as well.

I turned to everybody's best online friend, Google, for help. I tried Googling some different spellings and comparing the number of hits I got for each one:

- tieguanyin: 483,000

- tie guanyin: 776,000

- tie guan yin: 488,000

- ti kuan yin: 379,000

- tie kwun yin: 1,200,000

- tae guan yin: 39,000

And when I Googled "Iron Goddess of Mercy," I got 341,000 results.

I'm not sure how much this reflects how common any given spelling is, and how much it reflects how good Google is at guessing what you mean. The Wikipedia entry for Tieguanyin came up as the top result for almost all of those searches, even though the article doesn't use most of those spellings.

This led me to think, how can we expect to reach agreement on the spelling of tieguanyin's name when producers can't reach agreement on how much to oxidize it? But that's an entirely different question.

As with most ambiguous names, the best way to handle it is to pick a spelling and stick with it. You'll never change the rest of the world, but at least you'll be consistent, and that's what I've chosen to do in this book. My spellings of tea names might not be the same ones your favorite tea shop uses, but they'll be close enough to ask for the tea.

The tasting notes

At the end of each story, I've included an "about the tea" section. It talks about the tea in modern perspective: what it is, where it comes from, what it looks like, what it tastes like. The tasting notes are, of course, subjective. Not only that, but the tastes of teas vary. A $25.00 (US) per ounce ceremonial grade organic matcha will taste quite different from a $3.00 per ounce cooking grade matcha (and *very* different from a sweetened matcha for green tea lattes).

If you want to experience these teas as the stories describe them, I recommend selecting a tea shop with knowledgeable tea aficionados. No, let's just be blunt: tea freaks. Find a shop run by tea freaks. Tell them you want an Oriental Beauty oolong like the one you might have found in a Beipu market in 1931 and get out of their way.

Alternatively, ask those tea freaks for their favorite. That may spark some argument, but it's likely to get you some very good tea.

Prologue
The Origin of Tea
China, 2737 B.C.

As emperor of China, Shennong had a great deal of responsibility. His days were busy, but that did not keep him from his passions – most notably herbalism. He ruled an empire, introduced agriculture to his people, and invented acupuncture, but still had time to experiment with his beloved plants.

Millennia before the discovery of bacteria and our modern understanding of how diseases work, Shennong found that boiling water before drinking it somehow made it healthier. Even dangerous "bad" water became potable, although not always appetizing. Though he didn't understand the reasoning, his practice of boiling water made China a healthier place. It also led to one of his greatest contributions to the world: tea.

It had been a long, hard day. Shennong had been up since before dawn, handling matters of state. He was far from the capital, dealing with issues in a corner of his empire he had never before visited. While there, he had discovered an unfamiliar herb, and carefully collected a sample. Shennong had already cataloged over

100 plants and tested their medical properties. He was building his knowledge into what would eventually become the world's first pharmacopoeia.

He was a smart man, and he knew that some plants were toxic. Trying them out on someone else wasn't the right way to do it, though. Who could he trust to describe the effects accurately? So he used himself as a guinea pig, trying a huge variety of herbs and carefully noting the effect they had on his own body.

This particular herb had left him feeling queasy and unsteady. He called for a cup of water and went outside. His guards, although nervous, were used to Shennong's wanderings and fanned out around him, staying close enough to protect him, but far enough to respect his privacy. He found a beautiful old tree and settled beneath it, pulling his cloak tight against the chill in the autumn air. When his cook brought out the cup of freshly-boiled water, Shennong set it on the ground next to him and closed his eyes.

As Shennong relaxed, a light breeze blew some leaves from the tree, a healthy specimen of what would later be called *Camellia sinensis*, and several of the leaves settled into his cup. The dry leaves of fall generally carry little aroma, but as these leaves soaked up the hot water, Shennong noticed a pleasant fragrance rising from the cup.

He lifted the cup and examined it. The water had changed to a yellowish-green color. He lifted out one of the leaves, being careful not to burn his fingers. It was fairly slender with softly serrated edges. He crushed the leaf and smelled it carefully, then he dropped it back into the cup. He watched for another minute or so, and then lifted the cup to his lips and took a cautious sip.

Camellia sinensis is, of course, the tea plant. We generally see tea in carefully cultivated plantations, pruned to about waist height for easy picking. Left to grow wild, however, tea plants will grow into trees, and if there is any truth to the Shennong legend, the tree he sat under was probably 30 feet tall or more.

In Shennong's pharmacopoeia, he noted various plants along with their medicinal properties (if any), how to identify them, and how to prepare them for use as drinks, powders, or poultices. For poisonous plants, he noted the effects of the poison and listed antidotes where he could.

Tea would become the most widely consumed beverage in the world other than plain water, noted for its unique combination of energy (from the caffeine) and relaxing properties (from the L-Theanine). It was also listed by Shennong as the antidote to dozens of poisons.

And there's something else that tea brought us.

Stories.

The Japanese Tea Ceremony
Tea, Serenity, and Death
Japan, 1591

It is never wise to offend a daimyo, as Tea Master Sen no Rikyū discovers when his master, the daimyo Toyotomi Hideyoshi, commands him to commit seppuku (ritual suicide). Our story begins at Rikyū's home in Kyoto as he talks with one of his disciples, a Zen priest named Nanpō Sōkei.

"What will you do?" Sōkei asked as they entered the house.

"What can I do?" Rikyū responded. "I have dishonored the daimyo. He made his wishes very clear to me."

"I understand," Sōkei said quietly. "I meant, what will you do to prepare yourself? How can I be of service to you?"

Rikyū thought for a moment. Commissioning a statue of himself in the new temple certainly was neither humble nor appropriate, but that wasn't what had so upset Hideyoshi. It was the placement. He should have thought things through before placing the statue so that it looked down upon guests entering the temple. Nobody – even a statue – was entitled to look down upon the warlord.

Because of that one ill-advised decision, Rikyū had been commanded to take his own life.

He looked around his house. As the daimyo's tea master, he had luxurious quarters available to him in the castle, but he had instead chosen this small house. Décor was sparse and simple, as befitted the philosophy of *wabi-sabi* by which he lived his life. The only ornaments in the room were a *kakemono* (a hanging calligraphy scroll), a simple flower arrangement, and a *Raku* tea bowl.

"What was the first thing I taught you about *chanoyu*?" Rikyū asked, referring to the "way of tea" that he had spent his life perfecting. Sōkei smiled and recited a verse that was forever engraved upon his memory.

> *When tea is made with water drawn from the depths of mind*
> *Whose bottom is beyond measure,*
> *We really have what is called chanoyu.*

"Very good," Rikyū responded, returning the smile. "I have asked Daimyo Hideyoshi for permission to conduct one last *chanoyu*, one last tea ceremony, and he has granted me the honor. I must clear my mind and compose my thoughts. Would you do me the favor of inviting my guests for me?"

"Of course, master. Who shall I invite?"

Rikyū, wishing to limit the ceremony to four guests, gave Sōkei the names of three other disciples.

"Ask them to join us at the tearoom tomorrow at sunset," Rikyū told him.

After Sōkei left, Rikyū prepared a cup of tea and settled back to contemplate his life.

At the age of 69, he had already outlived many of his friends. He had been involved in the building of tearooms and temples. He had served as tea master to Japanese luminaries. He had studied Zen. He had been married and fathered children.

His legacy, though, was to be something different.

Sen no Rikyū had expanded upon the philosophy of *wabi-sabi*, which accepted and treasured transience, asymmetry, and imperfection. From it, he had formed *wabi-cha*, the philosophy of tea.

It was Rikyū that had simplified teahouses, removing unnecessary ornamentation. The aesthetic he preferred was one that made the inside and outside one. The artfully – but simply – arranged flowers in the tearoom were from the tea garden outside. A single *kakemono* scroll decorated the wall. The only implements present in the room were those required to prepare the tea.

He did not favor the highly decorated bowls that the Chinese used. His idea of the perfect *chawan* (tea bowl) was one that fit his hands and touched his heart. His favorite bowl had a chip out of the rim and a crack that he had carefully repaired himself. When presenting the bowl to a guest at a tea ceremony, he would carefully position the bowl so that the guest would see the chip and the crack, giving each person a chance to meditate upon their meaning and their contribution to the beauty inherent in the bowl.

The tea caddy from which he scooped the powdered matcha tea was similarly beautiful and similarly flawed.

The ladle, scoop, and whisk were all bamboo. They were carefully made, but transient. When they inevitably became stained, cracked, or broken, they were easy to replace and the new ones that took their place would be treasured no more and no less than the originals.

Rikyū believed that there were four important principles to *chanoyu*, the way of tea. *Wa kei sei jaku* was not only the core of the tea ceremony, but a representation of the principles to incorporate into daily life.

Wa (harmony) was his ultimate ideal. From harmony comes peace. Guest and host should be in harmony and man should strive for harmony with nature, rather than attempting to dominate nature. Incorporating *wa* into his impending *seppuku* would be one of Rikyū's greatest challenges.

Kei (respect) allows one to accept and understand others even when you do not agree with them. In a tea ceremony the guest must respect the host and the host must respect the guest, making them equals. The simplest vase should be treated as well as the most expensive, and the same politeness and purity of heart should be extended to your servant as to your master.

Sei (purity) is a part of the ritual of the tea ceremony, cleaning everything beforehand and wiping each vessel with a special cloth before using it. But that is only an outward reflection of the purity of the heart and soul that brings the harmony and respect. In accordance with *wabi-cha*, imperfection was to be prized here as well. To Rikyū, the ultimate expression of purity was the garden after he spent hours grooming it and several leaves settled randomly on the assiduously manicured walkway.

Finally, *Jaku* (tranquility) is the ultimate goal of enlightenment and selflessness. It is also the fresh beginning as you go back with new perspective to examine the way you have chosen to implement harmony, respect, and purity into your life.

Another of Rikyū's poems came to his mind as he thought about *chanoyu.*

> *Many though there be,*
> *Who with words or even hands*
> *Know the Way of Tea.*
> *Few there are or none at all,*
> *Who can serve it from the heart.*

This, then, was to be his goal: not to make his final tea ceremony a spectacle of the ego, but tea served from the heart. Achieving *wa kei sei jaku* was his principle goal in life. It would be his goal in death as well.

As each of his disciples arrived at the entrance to the garden, Rikyū greeted him with a bow and a hand-clasp. No words were spoken. When all five of them were present, he gestured down the path.

The garden and its path were impeccable. No servant had manicured the grounds for this ceremony. Rikyū had done it himself, gaining peace from the familiar ritual and humility from spending his day kneeling on the ground.

As his final guests started down the walk, the trees seemed to shudder and the lanterns to flicker even though not a breath of wind disturbed the grounds. The scent of carefully-selected incense wafted down the path, complimenting the jasmine planted in the garden rather than competing with it.

Rikyū had selected the time perfectly. The soft rose-colored light of dusk cast long shadows with soft edges that enhanced the already tranquil setting. The four guests walked up to the teahouse entrance and Rikyū separated himself from the group to circle around to the back.

Each guest in turn removed his shoes, bowed, and entered the teahouse on his knees through the low door. Each in turn took his place on the tatami mat floor along the wall of the tearoom and waited for Rikyū. The water was hot and the gentle aroma of the flowers arranged below the kakemono scroll filled the room.

Everything in the room was exactly in its place, looking like it had hundreds of times before. The only difference was a bag resting along the wall behind the tea master's usual position. Although curious, the guests carefully ignored it.

The tea master entered from the other door, performing his ritual with quiet and studied ease. Each implement was laid in its place, and each wiped down before use. Rikyū paused at that point and let his gaze fall upon each of his guests in turn as he recited:

> *Though you wipe your hands*
> *And brush off the dust and dirt*
> *From the tea vessels.*
> *What's the use of all this fuss*
> *If the heart is still impure?*

Carefully, he opened his tea caddy and placed three scoops of the bright green matcha tea powder into the bowl. Using the ritual cloth, he lifted the lid from the water vessel and set it aside. Steam rose from the roiling water within. He lifted the ladle and gently added water to the tea bowl. Resting the ladle on the edge of the water vessel, he lifted his *chasen* (whisk) and proceeded to mix and aerate the tea. When it was finished, he set down the whisk and carefully turned the bowl so that the "front" (the side with the chip and crack) faced Sōkei and presented him with the bowl.

As custom dictated, Sōkei drank the tea and then took a moment to admire the tea bowl before returning it to Rikyū.

Rikyū repeated the process for each of his four disciples.

After his bowl returned for the last time, each of his guests having had their tea, Rikyū made one last bowl for himself and set it on the tatami mat next to him. His guests looked at him, puzzled. The tea master always drank the final bowl of tea before setting it down. This was odd behavior for one who so strongly believed in the rituals of tea.

Rikyū bowed to his guests and reached behind him to get the bag they had been wondering about.

"Thank you for being here today," he said. "You have all been friends to me, and I have some small gifts to give. For each of you, one of the utensils from my tearoom and a *kakemono* scroll that I hope will be worthy to hang in your own home. They are simple scrolls produced by my own humble hands."

He turned to Sōkei and bowed, holding out his tea whisk and one of the scrolls.

"Sōkei, my friend, I have nothing left to teach you. I can only hope that I have taught you half as much as I have learned from you. I give to you my *chasen*. May your teachings whisk knowledge into the heads of your students just as this *chasen* whisks air into your tea."

Sōkei bowed and then took the gifts. He examined the whisk politely and placed it in his sleeve. He then unrolled the scroll. In simple, beautiful calligraphy it said *"wa kei sei jaku."* He examined it in silence for several minutes, pondering how each of the four elements were woven into this day: harmony, respect, purity, tranquility. He looked at Rikyū.

"You honor me greatly by giving me this scroll, master. As you have told me many times, no utensil ranks with the scroll in significance."

And on around the room Rikyū continued, giving away his tea scoop, his tea caddy with matcha still in it, and his ladle. With each utensil, he gave a *kakemono* similar to the one he gave Sōkei, all slightly different, all handmade by Rikyū.

Finally, he picked up his bowl and stared at it in silence. Sōkei stared as well, puzzled. Rikyū had already given a souvenir to each person present. What was he planning to do with his *chawan*? Rikyū held the bowl high and recited one of his most famous verses:

> *Tea is not but this.*
> *First you make the water boil,*
> *Then infuse the tea.*
> *Then you drink it properly.*
> *That is all you need to know.*

He drank deeply from the bowl and looked around the room at each of his friends. He then, very deliberately, shattered his prized *chawan* against his cast-iron teapot saying, "Never again shall this cup, polluted by the lips of misfortune, be used by man."

He bowed from his kneeling position, placing his forehead on the tatami mat. He held the position for ten long seconds, and then sat up straight, saying "Farewell, my friends."

His guests rose to their feet, and one by one they bowed and left the tea room. Sōkei was last to go, and Rikyū said to him, "Please do me the honor of staying."

Sōkei stood awkwardly, unsure of what to do. Rikyū stood and removed his tea gown, revealing the simple white death robes beneath. He carefully folded his tea gown and set it on the mat in front of him. He picked up the bag and drew forth a *wakizashi* and a *katana*. The knife and sword were simple; only polished steel and carefully wrapped handles with no adornments.

He set the bag down and walked over to Sōkei. He tried hard to keep his composure as he held out the *katana* in its plain leather *saya*. "Please," he said with wet eyes. "In case I do not have the strength to do this thing."

The priest looked at his mentor; his friend. If Rikyū did not kill himself cleanly, could he bring himself to administer the fatal blow? Honor demanded it. Friendship demanded it. He gently took the sword from Rikyū's hands.

"I accept your *katana*, but I shall not need it. You shall not need it. You can do what needs to be done."

Rikyū stepped back over to where he had lain his tea gown. He dropped to his knees and settled back. He placed the *wakizashi* across his knees, closed his eyes, and breathed deeply: once, twice, thrice. Eyes still closed, he lifted the *wakizashi* and pointed the blade at his abdomen. Opening his eyes, he gazed at the dagger and recited the death poem that he had written.

Welcome to thee,
O sword of eternity!
Through Buddha
And through Daruma alike
Thou hast cleft thy way.[1]

He lifted his eyes and looked at Sōkei, who drew the *katana* from its *saya* and stepped behind him.

One last deep breath, and he felt the last of the stress leaving him. It was time to do what honor demanded. A faint smile came to his lips as he plunged home the blade. He was at peace.

Sōkei stood behind Rikyū's still body for a moment, finally allowing the tears to come. Unseeing, he dropped the katana. He picked up the *chasen* and scroll he had been given and left the tearoom without looking back.

From the teachings of Rikyū came several schools of chanoyu, the Way of Tea. Even now, 400 years after his death, they still hold memorial services for him every year. The ritual of the tea ceremony remains virtually unchanged. Even though matcha tea is integral to the ceremony, the center of chanoyu remains Rikyū's core values of harmony, respect, purity, and tranquility.

---

[1] There are several versions of Rikyū's death poems (some say he wrote two: one in Chinese and one in Japanese). The one I have chosen is the translation by Kakuzo Okakura in *The Book of Tea*.

Matcha

Matcha had already been around for centuries when Rikyū developed the ceremony. Originally, the dried leaves were powdered using a hand-carved millstone designed for tea leaves. The millstone had a hole in the top where dried tea leaves were inserted, and a vertical wooden shaft in the lower stone kept it centered. Grooves inside the millstone moved the ground-up leaves out to a dish or bowl carved in a second stone underneath.

The leaves used for making matcha are typically buds and new leaves, and the plants are shaded for some period of time (usually several weeks) before picking. They are dried inside or in the shade, always avoiding direct sunlight.

Not all tea shops carry matcha powder. It's a specialized tea with a limited following outside of Japan. If you are looking for good matcha, it is best to find a tea house that serves it. This allows you to watch the process, and to sample the matcha that they sell.

Good matcha should be fresh (check the "best by" date on the can, if there is one) and bright green. Dark, drab shades of green indicate low grade matcha. It should smell fresh. If it doesn't have much smell, it won't have much taste either.

Tea is a very personal thing. Nobody can tell you what tastes good to you. The "right" way for me to enjoy a particular tea could be quite different than the "right" way for you to enjoy that same tea. To Rikyū, the tea ceremony was not about what made your matcha taste the best. It was all about using the ritual to clear your mind and help you to see things more clearly. It was about achieving harmony, respect, purity, and tranquility.

Outside of the ceremony, however, I would argue that your way of relaxing is the right way of relaxing, whether it means making a bowl of matcha, sitting on your front porch with a steaming hot cup of Earl Grey, preparing a delicate silver needle tea to enjoy with a friend, or laying back in the bathtub with a fragrant jasmine green tea. Tea should be a pleasure, not a chore, and the tea ceremony is about sharing that pleasure with your friends and guests.

Any shop that sells matcha should also sell the four main implements used to prepare it. You don't need all four, but here's what you should look for if you want the full experience:

The Chawan (Matcha Bowl)

You use the chawan to prepare your matcha, and also to drink it. A chawan is a highly personal item, and most aficionados shun "perfect" bowls, instead preferring handmade bowl with irregularities and personalities. Some have a summer bowl, shallow and lightweight, and a winter bowl, deep and heavy. It is not at all unusual to name your chawan, or have the creator or your tea master name it for you.

You can certainly acquire a chawan for $20.00 (US) or less. You can also spend hundreds of dollars for a beautiful handmade chawan, and thousands for an antique owned by a well-known tea master. It's entirely up to you.

The Chasen (Whisk)

To make matcha properly, you must have a proper whisk. Chasen are not expensive. Five or ten U.S. dollars will get you a perfectly good one. It should be made of bamboo, and you should rinse it thoroughly after every use and set it aside to dry. Chasen are designed to stand upright on the base, keeping the whisk end clean and letting it drip dry.

The Chashaku (Scoop)

You don't really need a chashaku to make matcha. Any little spoon will work. The bamboo chashaku, however, is designed to scoop the right amount of matcha out of a tiny container without having to lift or tilt that container. If you find a matcha "set" for sale, it will probably include a chashaku along with a bowl and whisk.

The Chaki (Caddy)

There are different caddies for "thin tea" and "thick tea," and you can find chaki made from ceramic, wood, or bamboo. They have different styles, different lids, different finishes, and many different names. Most people just getting into matcha simply use the container the matcha comes in (usually a small can) as their chaki until they acquire one that has some meaning to them.

Serving Matcha

Matcha is typically made in one of two ways, known as koicha ("thick tea") and usucha ("thin tea"). The preparation is very similar. If you have participated in a Japanese tea ceremony, you probably drank thick tea. If you had matcha with a friend or at a tea shop, it was most likely thin tea.

With either one, you start by warming the bowl. Pour in some hot water, swirl it around, and then dump it out.

Then add the matcha powder. If your matcha has been in a humid environment, or if it's been stored for a while, it may be clumpy. In this case, run it through a sieve first. For thin tea, use a bit less than 2 grams of tea, which is roughly 1½ heaping chashaku scoops. For thick tea, use about four times that amount.

After the powder, add about 2½ ounces (75 ml) of hot water.

Do not use boiling water! Matcha can be bitter, and boiling water will make it far more bitter, ruining the flavor. Ideally, water should be in the 165-185°F (75-85°C) range.

If you are making thin tea, whisk it briskly until it is well mixed and there's a good layer of foam on top. Be careful if you're using a chawan with a rough surface, as you may end up making quite a mess.

Thick tea, usually made with very high-grade matcha powder, shouldn't be whisked to a froth. Whisk more gently until the drink is of even consistency – more like syrup than tea – and serve immediately. Despite having so much more tea powder, thick tea usually tastes milder and less bitter than thin tea.

You can also use matcha for cooking. It is used in green tea ice cream (the main reason I wanted to go to Japanese restaurants as a child), and you can also use it to flavor and color everything from cupcakes and tiramisu to yogurt and pancakes.

Tieguanyin
The Iron Goddess of Mercy
China, 1761

It was the reign of the Qianlong Emperor, the sixth emperor of the Qing Dynasty in China, but our story concerns no emperors, warlords, or nobles. It is just a tale of a humble farmer by the name of Wei.

Wei lived in Anxi Country in the Chinese province of Fujian. People there were struggling with hard times. Fujian, they say, is eight parts mountain, one part water, and one part farmland. Wei's tiny village was no exception. He and his neighbors grew what they could. A bit of wheat, a bit of rice, and a few sweet potatoes were enough for most of them to get by.

Their favorite crop was tea. They worked hard to produce good tea, using the complex oolong production style. Their process wasn't bad but the result was usually mediocre, as it came from poor stock.

"Oh, well," they used to say. "You can't get silk from an earthworm."

Each week, Wei would go to market in the city. Each week, he passed an old temple that had fallen into disrepair. The pathway was overgrown, the gates had fallen, and it appeared that nobody had worshipped there in a very long time. It was such a part of the scenery that Wei walked by it without even seeing it.

Like the rest of his village, Wei was a Buddhist. It's difficult to describe how Buddhism works to Westerners like us, as the Buddha himself isn't considered a god but an enlightened being. What we often refer to as gods and goddesses in Buddhism, actual Buddhists would call bodhisattvas. The temple Wei passed each week was built for the Bodhisattva Guanyin, whom you or I might call the Goddess of Mercy.

One particular day – a day that would become a major turning point for Wei, Wei's village, and lovers of tea everywhere – Wei stopped on the road to rest. Not that stopping on the road was an unusual occurrence. The trip was long and Wei was not as young as he used to be. On this very notable day, however, he stopped right at the pathway to the temple of Guanyin.

After Wei set down his heavy load, he pushed back his hat and wiped the sweat from his forehead. What used to be the temple's garden was surrounded by a small rock wall, more decorative than functional. It would do no good at keeping out deer or rodents, and in its current tumbledown state, even a rabbit could hop right through in several places.

Once, the flowers and cherry trees of the garden had been carefully-tended, but that was long ago. The undergrowth almost completely obscured the path, bushes had grown tall and scraggly, and the unpruned cherry trees blocked the sun to the flowers. *At least*, he thought, *the wall provides a place to sit and the trees give me shade.*

He looked down the pathway, wiped his sleeve across his forehead again, and thought about the temple.

Guanyin is the Goddess of Mercy, he thought. Okay, perhaps he called her a bodhisattva rather than a goddess, but he was, after all, Chinese, and neither goddess nor bodhisattva is a Chinese word, so I shall use the more familiar word in my telling of Wei's story.

It is not seemly that we should treat Guanyin's temple with such disrespect, he continued to himself. *We should show … well … mercy.*

He picked up his wares and continued to market, but his moment of epiphany (or dare I say, enlightenment?) stuck with him throughout the day. The following week, he brought some old gardening tools with him and stashed them beside the pathway on his way to market. He hurried through the selling of what little he had to sell and the buying of what little he could afford to buy, and then he headed home.

When Wei reached the temple, he retrieved his tools and began clearing the path. Carefully, he pruned back the bushes that encroached on the pathway. Thoughtfully, he trimmed the tree branches that overhung the walk. Delicately, he pulled the weeds from the path itself. Soon, the sky began to redden as the sun fell in the west, and he secured his tools behind the rock wall and went home, a bit disappointed that he had cleared only the beginning of the path.

Over the following weeks, Wei repeated the process. Sometimes he would clear the plants. Sometimes he would fix the flat rocks and fill in gaps to smooth the path. Sometimes he would leave the path alone for an evening and work on the wall. He made a special trip with a friend from the village to fix the gate.

This continued until the path was clear all the way to the temple entrance. Pleased with his progress, he lit a candle and stepped into the temple itself.

The sorry state of the exterior was nothing compared to the disrepair of the inside. Webs occupied the corners of the room, and spiders occupied the webs. Dust was everywhere. The offering bowl was reduced to ragged shards, and vines crept in the windows. A mouse skittered across the floor, and a snake watched hungrily from behind the altar. But Wei noticed none of it. All of his attention was drawn to the statue of Guanyin.

There she sat! The center of the temple was dominated by the statue of a beautiful maiden meditating. In her lap she held a fish basket. Although the statue was dirty and old, it was unbroken and the fine details of her necklace and her Tang Dynasty clothing were clear. Wei thought he could see sadness on that lovely face, and it nearly broke his heart.

He stood staring at Guanyin for many minutes, finally breaking his reverie to look about the room. To one side was a painting of Guanyin with a child on each side and a white parrot above. A beetle crawled across the frame. Even the painting looked sad, he thought.

Wei was touched by the experience and vowed that he would get rid of that melancholy look. He continued coming back each week on his way home from market. On one visit, he brought a stick long enough to take down the spider webs. Of course, he carefully took the spiders outside without harming them. Guanyin is, after all, the Goddess of Mercy.

The next week, he brought a broom and swept out the temple. The next, he delicately dusted the statue itself. He found the nest the mice had built and moved it outside. The snake, he scooted out the door with the broom. This had to be repeated several times as snakes can be stubborn once they've chosen a home.

The next time he stopped at the temple, he looked at the shattered bowl in front of Guanyin's statue. He carefully gathered the pieces of the broken offering bowl in the sleeve of his robe and took them home. He set the pieces on his table and studied them. Wei was a simple farmer. He didn't have the skills to repair the bowl. But perhaps he knew someone who did.

Wei once again gathered up the bowl fragments and carried them to the home of his good friend Wang, the potter. Wang invited Wei into his home and went immediately to the teapot. After all, when a friend visits, it is important to serve them tea.

As the water heated, Wei began to tell Wang about the temple. Wang listened as he carefully measured out the leaves. At first, the tale did not interest him much, for China is filled with old temples and roadside altars. Some are well-kept. Some are not.

As large bubbles began to form and rise through the water (the Chinese people call this stage "fish eyes"), Wang put the tea on to steep. When Wei started to tell him about the offering bowl Wang's ears perked up.

"I do not know how to fix the bowl," Wei told him, "and I do not have the money to buy one."

"Let me look," Wang said, and Wei spread out the pieces before him. Wang became so engrossed in studying the broken bowl that he almost forgot to pour the tea. He was so distracted that he hardly noticed the muddy flavor and the bitterness of their tea.

When you can rarely afford to buy good tea, you soon become accustomed to poor tea.

"Can you repair this," Wei asked anxiously, "or perhaps make another one like it?"

"Where will you get the money to pay for it?" Wang responded. "I am very busy and must make many bowls to sell so that I can feed my family. And Guanyin's temple is your project, not mine."

"You are my friend, Wang. When you were sick last summer, who brought tea and rice for you and your wife? When the monsoon rains came early two seasons ago, who helped you to make a ditch to drain your wheat field and irrigate your rice properly?"

"You are right, Wei. I am sorry. Friends help their friends. I shall make you a proper bowl. I cannot do it today, and maybe not for a couple of weeks, but I will make a bowl that you will be proud to give to Guanyin."

And so things went. Wei replaced the offering bowl with the one that Wang made him. He pruned the trees. He found an inexpensive incense burner and set it in a nook on the wall. He took a pitcher of water and washed the statue. He kept the pathway clear. He even planted some flowers. And every week he lit incense and meditated before he left.

One day, Wei walked into the temple and realized he had done everything he could do. All of the little things were repaired. Everything was clean. The incense was burning and someone – he did not know who – had placed an offering in the bowl. He looked at the statue of Guanyin and thought he detected a trace of a smile. Just a tiny bit. Just at the corner of her mouth. But he didn't see the sadness he had seen before.

There may actually have been a hint of smile on the statue's face, or Wei may have been imagining it. It really didn't matter, though. It brought a real smile to Wei's face. There's a special kind of happiness we get from doing things for others, things that bring us no personal benefit. That is what Wei felt as he walked home that afternoon.

That night, as Wei slept, he had a vivid dream. Not like our normal dreams, where things have soft edges and little detail and we forget them as soon as we wake. This dream was crystal clear, and felt like he was actually experiencing it.

Wei stood on the shore of an ocean where a mighty storm was raging. He was on a rock looking down at the powerful waves crashing against the shore. The wind whipped the spray into his face and threatened to knock him from his precarious perch. Although it was daytime, the dark clouds above hid the sun from him, making everything look like it was drawn in charcoal.

He seemed to actually feel the sea water on his skin, hear the howl of the wind and the roar of the surf, smell the salt in the air. Never had he experienced a dream with such clarity, and it made him nervous.

He fell to one knee and braced himself against the wind so that it wouldn't sweep him into the surf booming against the sharp outcroppings below him. As he knelt there, the clouds parted far out over the water and he saw a beam of sunshine fight its way through. Where it hit the water, the head of an enormous sea dragon breached the surface of the sea, and the furious storm-whipped waves began to calm around its mighty neck. As more of the dragon crested, Wei saw someone standing on its back, wearing flowing white robes.

As the dragon approached, the calm water and the beam of light came with it. Soon, Wei could make out the woman riding upon the dragon. It was Guanyin, carrying a willow branch in her right hand and a jar of clear water in her left. Although water coursed from the back of the sea dragon, Guanyin's hair and robes were dry. On her face was an expression so serene, so calm, that Wei did not fear the monstrous beast that towered high over the shore. Guanyin stood effortlessly, her dry feet showing no signs of slipping on the wet scales of the dragon's back.

When the dragon approached his rock, Wei was encompassed by the beam of light. The crashing of the waves ceased and the world around him suddenly felt like it was painted in delicate watercolor. Tranquility settled over him, and he rose to his feet to find himself looking into the eyes of Guanyin. He fell back to his knees and bowed his head.

"Rise," she told him. He stood awkwardly, intimidated by her presence and the head of the dragon looming over him, water dripping from the barbels alongside the fearsome mouth.

She studied him for a long moment before she spoke. He kept his head down, but could not stop himself from looking at her.

"You are a good man, Wei," she said. "You have worked long and hard to restore my temple, and you have shown me great respect. What would you ask from me as a reward?"

He responded without stopping to think. "I did what I did because it needed to be done. I did not fix your temple because I sought reward. I fixed it because it was the right thing to do."

"I know that," the goddess responded. For the first time, Wei saw a smile on her face, and it brought such joy to his heart that he almost interrupted her. Luckily, he held back, for it is not wise to interrupt the gods. But what reward could compare with bringing a smile to the face of the Goddess of Mercy? No man could ask for more.

"Had you done this for a reward," she continued, "I would not be inclined to give you one. But your motives are pure and enlightened. Kindness deserves kindness, and for that reason, I shall reward you.

"You did not select a gift, so I have selected one for you. You shall find it behind the temple, shadowed by the large bear-shaped rock. It holds the key to your future and your village's future, so treat it with care and respect."

He bowed his head again as the dragon pulled back from the rock upon which he stood. The clouds dissipated from the sky, and the sea became smooth as glass. A single yellow butterfly danced before him as the dragon swam away, gradually disappearing under the water.

Wei stood on the rock, overcome with joy. Slowly, the vision faded and he settled into a deep dreamless sleep.

When Wei awoke in the morning, he lay quietly in his bed, serene and rested. Then the dream came back to him. He leapt out of bed and rushed through his morning routine. He felt no hunger, and took only a moment to eat a half-bowl of rice, barely tasting it as he ate.

He rushed to the temple. How different it looked! The stone wall looked sturdy and solid. Flowers were beginning to bloom in the rays of sunlight that streamed through the neatly-pruned cherry trees, which were showing signs of blooming themselves. The entrance to the temple was inviting, clean, tidy.

Without even pausing to enter the temple and light incense, Wei stepped from the path and circled around behind. He hadn't ventured here before. It was still wild. A rivulet of water burbled happily down the steep slope, and only a small area was flat and level. In that small area stood the bear-shaped rock that Guanyin had referred to, taller than Wei himself.

He looked eagerly in the rock's shadow, not knowing what to expect, and saw nothing but dirt, rocks, and a pathetic little sprig of a plant.

I see nothing, he thought. My treasure must be buried.

But as Wei kneeled to start digging, something about the sapling caught his eye. The deep green of the leaves and their slightly jagged edges looked familiar. It was a tea plant! Small, undernourished, with only a few leaves, but a tea plant nonetheless. He dug it up and carefully transplanted it into his garden at home.

For days and weeks, he watered it, tended it, fertilized it, all the while not quite sure if this tiny plant was really his reward from the goddess. The scraggly plant grew quickly into a thick healthy bush. The trunk grew strong and thick; the leaves glossy and bright. He picked a leaf and crushed it between his fingers. The aroma was strong and sweet. It was time.

Carefully, he selected a handful of delicate new buds and the young leaves next to them. He laid them out in the sun to wither, and went to tell his friend Wang about his prize. Wang came back to see the tea bush, and they took the leaves into the house to cool.

"Should I go to the city and find a tea master to help me prepare this properly?" Wei asked his friend.

"No," said Wang. "Guanyin gave *you* this tea plant. Meditate as the leaves cool. Clear your mind, and then follow your instincts."

And so he did. He followed the same process that he always used with the scruffy tea plants that he and his neighbors grew. Tossing, a bit of oxidizing, fixing; he dedicated the next day to working with his prized leaves.

He rolled the leaves as oolong tea makers did – and still do. Not being very skilled at it, he ended up not with neat little balls, but with little curled-up tadpole shapes, which he roasted very lightly. Over the next two days, they dried hard as he looked on impatiently. At last, the leaves appeared ready.

Excited, Wei fetched one of his most prized possessions: a beautiful black iron teapot. He took a small scoop of the leaves and dropped them into the teapot and they made sharp "ping" sounds, almost like iron pieces tumbling into the iron pot. He rushed to get Wang and some of his neighbors. They looked at him dubiously as he chattered on about the visit from Guanyin in his dream. They passed around one of his dried leaves and looked it over uncertainly.

Then he poured the hot water over the leaves in his teapot, and the aroma of the tea struck them. They rushed in to look, to smell, and – when the tea was finished steeping – to taste.

The tea was magical. It had a rich amber color and a bold taste with overtones of honey and spice. They held the liquid in their mouths and it felt smooth and light. The taste lingered long after the tea was swallowed, and it brought what could only be called an energizing calm to the villagers. All of the tea they had ever produced before suddenly seemed inadequate and drab.

Because of the hard dried leaves and their ringing sound when dropped on iron or steel, Wei called the tea tieguanyin, which we translate today as Iron Goddess of Mercy.

As Wei's tea bush flourished, he took cuttings for his neighbors, his friends, and his own farm. All of the other tea plants in the village were slowly replaced, and he taught everyone in the village how to produce his special tea. Soon there was enough tieguanyin to take to market, and the reputation of the tea spread like fire.

The poor village prospered and expanded, but Wei was always there to remind them to take time for Guanyin's temple. Together, they expanded the garden around the temple, lovingly planted with the most beautiful and fragrant flowers, the most luscious fruits, and of course, the goddess' own tea bushes.

They sculpted a streambed for the water flowing down the slopes behind the temple. They directed the water around the bear-shaped rock and past the temple to the front, where the garden filled with the tinkling sound of water over rocks, and made a pool in front, which they filled with koi and lilies. In that magic way that ponds have, it filled itself with frogs, who added their music to the sound of the stream.

Drinking a cup of tieguanyin there made the garden seem brighter and the tea taste better. Life was not always easy in the village, but it was never as hard as it had been before Wei began his work on Guanyin's temple.

Does that temple still stand? I don't know. If so, I think you'll agree that the statue of Guanyin upon that alter must now be smiling as tea lovers the world over enjoy the rich ambrosia that we call tieguanyin.

About Iron Goddess of Mercy

Tieguanyin, like most oolongs, is a complex tea to create. A simplified version of the process might look like this:

1. Picking – usually done early in the day when it is sunny

2. Sun drying ("withering") – Done before sunset the same day as the picking

3. Cooling ("cool green") – Done overnight, along with the tossing

4. Tossing ("shake green")

5. Partial oxidation – Done the day after picking

6. Fixing

7. Rolling/kneading

8. Drying

9. Roasting/curing

The whole process takes two or three days, and it is well worth it.

A group of tea people have started a tradition we call Teaku Tuesday, where we write a haiku about tea once a week and post it on Twitter with the hashtag #TeakuTuesday. You'll also find our teaku on other social media from time to time. The first teaku that

I wrote about tieguanyin said nothing about the flavor or the aroma. It simply expressed the draw that this tea has for me.

> *Endless tea choices*
> *Yet once again here I sit*
> *drinking tieguanyin*

Tieguanyin is one of my favorite teas. Despite being surrounded by other options, I often default to tieguanyin when I can't decide what I want.

Not all Iron Goddess of Mercy tea is created equal. It is now made not only throughout Fujian province, but in much of the rest of China, and Taiwan as well. Different producers use different varietals of the tea plant, pick at different times of year, and use different levels of oxidation, which produces a wide variety of flavors and aromas – all with the same name.

Tieguanyin comes in tightly-rolled balls. As you steep the tea, the balls will open up into full *Camellia sinensis* leaves. I prefer to brew my tieguanyin in a clear steeper so that I can watch the process: the agony of the leaves, as it is known.

There is no clear consensus on water temperature for tieguanyin tea, but I generally prefer to brew it like a green tea, using water at about 175°F (80°C). Use about a teaspoon of leaf for every cup of water, and steep it for 2½ to 3 minutes.

One of the wonderful things about tieguanyin – and many other oolongs – is that you can reuse the leaves. In fact, I rather prefer the second steeping to the first. For each additional cup of tea, add about 30 seconds to the steep time. I usually use my leaves four or five times, but many people get seven cups from their leaves – very appropriate, as seven is considered a lucky number in China.

Earl Grey
This Water Sucks!
England, 1806

The footman opened the front door at Howick Hall for Charles Grey II and took his cloak.

"Welcome home, Lord Howick. Would you care for some tea?"

"I would love some tea. I will take it in the drawing room after I change out of my travel clothes. It's been a long ride from London."

"Very well, sir. I'll call the valet for you."

When Charles walked into the drawing room, his wife was there to greet him.

"Welcome home dear! I do miss you on these interminable London trips."

"I miss you as well, Mary, but the trips will only get worse now."

"Now that you're First Lord of the Admiralty, you mean? I hope you shan't let that go to your head," she smiled.

The conversation was interrupted by the arrival of the tea service, which was laid out quickly and unobtrusively. The Lord and Lady sat and she poured a cup for each of them.

"Bah!" he exclaimed after his first sip. "A couple of weeks in London and I forget about how foul our water is here at Howick Hall."

"It's not that bad, Charles. It's just that we have so much limestone here!"

"Perhaps all that lime is not so bad when you're accustomed to it, but how can we serve this to our guests next week? There will be close to a hundred people at the soirée celebrating my elevation to First Lord and father being made the first Earl Grey. The lime taste in this tea is beyond off-putting."

"Can we just bring in water from London for the party?"

"I suppose we could, Mary, but that only takes care of the immediate problem. I want a long-term solution."

"Is there nothing we can do to our own water to correct it?"

"I've spoken to the cook and she is at her wits' end."

"Don't you know any tea experts you could consult? What about that Chinese fellow in Edinburgh? He imports tea, as I recall."

"The mandarin, Chen? I had rather forgotten about him. I did help his son out of an unpleasant situation back in ought-three, so he owes me a rather large favor. Wonderful idea, Mary!"

After dinner, Lord Howick penned a letter to Chen. He closed it up, added his seal, and handed it to the butler.

"Give this to the coachman and have him head out to Edinburgh at first light tomorrow, would you, Tom?"

"Certainly, sir."

The next four days were occupied with preparations for the celebration. The servants bustled about the household, and temporary hired help set up tents in the garden area for serving. The Greys stayed busy planning the festivities, but Charles thought about the mandarin every time he had a cup of tea.

Finally, horse hooves and coach wheels crunched in the gravel in front. The footman and houseboy unloaded a large chest as the coachman helped an old Chinese man out of the coach. Lord Howick came out and warmly greeted the mandarin.

"Chen, it is good to see you again. Thank you very much for coming!"

"I appreciate the opportunity to repay my debt, Sir Charles."

"Please, come and have dinner with us."

"I have eaten as we rode, Sir Charles. We do not have much time. I should begin my work."

"As you wish. Let me show where you can work. They have set up a space adjoining the kitchen."

The two men chatted as they walked to the kitchen. The servants followed, lugging Chen's heavy chest. As they walked through the halls, the housekeeper joined the procession. When they entered the kitchen, the cook kept the kitchen maids and scullery maid back out of the way as the footman and houseboy carried the unwieldy chest into an alcove off of the kitchen.

The cook scurried along with them and indicated a spot in the corner of the room. The chest hit the ground with a thump.

"Gently, please," the old mandarin said as he shooed them away from the chest and bent down to unbuckle the straps.

The room was warm from the great cooking fire on the other wall, where a cast-iron pot of stew bubbled. Scraps of lamb and vegetables littered the table, and the smell from the stew permeated the room. Extra lanterns were unobtrusively positioned to light the alcove, and they had moved in a small worktable. Next to the table was a wooden crate covered in Chinese writing. The top had been pried off to reveal a bale of aromatic black tea leaves.

Chen didn't notice any of this as he focused on his precious chest.

The footman gasped as Chen lifted the lid. A clever arrangement of riveted metal pieces tied a series of trays together. When closed, they folded together in the chest, each tray forming the lid to the one underneath it. When opened, they spread out to display an enormous selection of jars and vials containing liquids, powders, leaves, roots, and dried flowers. Another tray set on rails inside the chest contained glassware, sprayers, cups, pots, kettles, tongs, measuring spoons, droppers, and a well-packed balance scale.

Charles smiled as the servants gawked at the chest.

"May I have some water, please?" asked Chen.

"I can make you some tea, sir," the cook interjected.

"No, thank you. Just a cup of plain water, please."

The cook handed him a cup and he sniffed it delicately. He wrinkled his nose, closed his eyes, and sipped the water. He swished it around his mouth and swallowed.

"I do not need to drink your tea to see the problem, Sir Charles. There is much – what do you call it? – calcium in the water."

"Yes. Or as we usually call it, lime. Can we remove it?"

"You think only of changing the water. I think differently. The water is what it is. Instead of trying to make it something it is not, let us prepare a tea blend that will harmonize with it. Instead of working against nature, let us work with nature."

Charles chuckled.

"I trust you, Chen, but you are right that we do not have much time. Can you find your harmony with nature in a few days?"

"If I may impose upon you for a mattress on the floor here, I shall not leave this room until you have a tea that you can serve without shame."

Charles nodded at the housekeeper, who grabbed the houseboy's arm and hustled off to fetch bedding. He then walked over to the tea crate.

"This is the tea that we normally prepare here," he told Chen.

Chen picked up a bit of leaf and examined it. He crushed some under his nose and inhaled deeply, then raised an eyebrow at Charles.

"Fujian black tea?"

"Quite right."

"This will do."

He turned his back on Charles and began removing equipment from the chest. For Chen, Charles might as well have ceased to exist. The collection of carefully-organized gear began to move to the table. Most of it was ordinary, and Charles showed little interest. The balance scale, however, was a beautiful and intricate piece of machinery, and Chen had to shoo him away from it. Eventually, Charles wandered off to let Chen perform his magic.

"Do you think he can do it?" Mary asked when Charles met her in the drawing room.

"He certainly seems to know what he's doing – and he doesn't want me in the way," Charles replied with a wry smile.

"You're not much used to being told what to do in your own home, are you, dear?"

"Not much, but I have to trust him."

Several times over the course of the day Charles went down to the kitchen to check on Chen. This made the cook and the kitchen maids nervous, but the mandarin paid him no attention at all. Each time he was surrounded by tasting cups filled with various tea-like concoctions, decoctions, and infusions. Each time his alcove was a potpourri of exotic aromas.

The scents spanned the spectrum. Floral ranged from delicate jasmine to earthy black lotus. There were commonplace herbs and spices like ginger, sage, and cinnamon alongside their rare and expensive counterparts like fennel pollen and saffron. Dried berries, cocoa powder, and even white truffles were arranged along the table.

After the third kitchen visit, Charles decided he could watch in silence no longer.

"Do you have a cup of bedtime tea for me, Chen?"

"I have eliminated many options, Sir Charles. Each draws me closer to a solution. None yet produces the cup of tea that you seek. Go. Rest. We shall see where I am tomorrow morning."

Holding his impatience in check, Charles bid Chen goodnight and headed off to bed.

It seemed like he had barely closed his eyes when Charles was awakened to the sound of a loud argument in the hallway. The door opened, and Mary clutched the bedding to her chest as Charles sat up in bed.

The lady's maid was first through the door, working hard to hold it closed. Chen was using all of his weight to push her backward while clutching a teapot (full) and teacup (empty) to his chest. The valet was attempting to stop Chen, and all three were yelling over top of each other.

"What the bloody hell?" Charles thundered.

All three of the intruders went silent, standing awkwardly in the doorway as Chen moved the hot teapot away from his body.

"The sun isn't even up yet, Lady Howick is frightened out of her wits, and YOU ARE DISRUPTING MY HOUSEHOLD!" Charles took a deep breath, and then continued slightly more calmly. "Now who is going to tell me what's going on?"

All three began speaking at once.

"Stop," said Charles. He pointed at his valet. "You."

The valet closed his eyes, opened them, and said "I had just begun preparing your shaving equipment when this one," he scowled at Chen, "strolled down the hallway like he owned the place and started into your bedchamber. Miss Howe went to stop him and that's what started the fracas."

"Is that right, Miss Howe?" Charles looked at his wife's maid, who cringed and nodded her head vigorously.

"So, Chen. What is so bloody important that you feel the need to burst into my chambers before the sunrise has a chance to?"

"May I, Sir Charles?" Chen asked quietly, pointing at Lord Howick's bedside table. Charles nodded, and the valet and lady's maid moved out of Chen's way.

Chen walked wordlessly to the bedside table and set the empty cup down on it. He pulled a small screen out of the sleeve of his robe and set it over the cup. Next, he settled the lid back on the hot teapot and brushed the spilled tea from the front of his robe. Carefully, he poured some tea through the screen, which captured some errant leaves and prevented them from entering the teacup.

Releasing the bedding she was clutching, Mary sat up. "What is that fragrance?"

The smell of hot black tea filled the bedchamber, but there was something else....

Charles reached for the cup, and Chen removed the screen. Mary and her husband leaned over together, breathing deeply of the steam coming from the tea.

"It smells a bit citrusy, but not like it has lemon in it," Mary said. She glanced at the tray, and then at Chen. "Where is the milk and sugar?"

Chen grimaced. "Please. Try tea the Chinese way first. No milk."

Charles sipped the tea and raised his eyebrows quizzically at Chen, who looked at him anxiously. The tea didn't have the sour tones of lemon or the bitterness of grapefruit, but there was most certainly a citrus note, and he didn't notice the taste of calcium at all.

"That is absolutely wondrous! Mary, you must taste this. Chen, what have you done? Was that made with Howick Hall water?"

Chen looked at Lady Howick, who was blowing carefully on the hot beverage, and then back at Charles.

"We needed something that would be harmonious with both the water and the tea," he began. "Many flowers I tried, and herbs, and spices. Even berries did not accomplish what I desired. Then I tried the essential oil of the bergamot orange."

"You put orange juice in the tea?" Mary asked, taking another sip.

"Not juice. Essential oil from the skin. And this fruit is not an orange. It is grown in the south of Italy. It is called bergamot for the name of a town."

Charles took the cup back from Mary and sipped again.

"Chen, you have done exactly what I had hoped you could do. This is wonderful. Do you have enough of this oil to make a large batch of this tea?"

"I have only one vial with me, Sir Charles, but I believe I have enough to treat perhaps five pounds of tea for you. I can give your cook instructions for its preparation and send you more of the oil when I return to Edinburgh."

"That would be outstanding, Chen." He turned to his valet. "When he has finished preparing the tea, please show him to a guest chamber and let him get some sleep."

The party was a rousing success, as was the tea. Charles' father became the 1st Earl Grey, and died the following year at age 78, at which point Charles became the 2nd Earl Grey.

Charles was a whirlwind of activity within the Whig Party, and became Prime Minister of the United Kingdom in 1830. Among the accomplishments of his administration were Parliamentary reform and the abolition of slavery in the British Empire.

His special blend soon became known as Earl Grey's tea, and despite all of his accomplishments, black tea with bergamot has become his best-known legacy. Earl Grey tea enjoys quite possibly the highest name recognition of any tea in Britain and its former colonies. Mary has been immortalized in leaf as well, through Lady Grey tea, a popular variant with added lemon and orange.

About Earl Grey Tea

Jacksons of Piccadilly says that their original recipe for Earl Grey tea remains virtually unchanged since 1930. Twinings introduced theirs in 1831 and didn't change the recipe until 2011. And we can rest assured that 350 years from now, when Captain Jean-Luc Picard dictates his captain's log for stardate 42609.1, he'll be sipping on a cup of tea. Earl Grey. Hot.

Today, the market is swimming in a bewildering array of Earl Grey teas. Many are just called Earl Grey. Many have variations of the name, like Earl Greyer, Earl Grey Supreme, or Aromatic Earl Grey. There are organic Earl Greys, fair trade Earl Greys, and kosher Earl Greys. There is Earl Grey made with green tea ("Earl Green"), white tea ("Earl White"), and rooibos ("Earl Red"). Start adding more ingredients and you have Lady Grey, Lavender Earl Grey, Citrus Earl Grey, Sapphire Earl Grey, and Post-Apocalyptic Earl Grey (more on that later).

At its core, Earl Grey tea is simply black tea with bergamot oil. Traditionally, it was Chinese black tea, but virtually every black tea is used for Earl Grey now. It has become the archetypical British tea, so I'd recommend preparing it as you would any other British black tea.

The English do take their tea seriously. In fact, ISO (the International Organization for Standardization) even has a formal standard for preparing a cup of tea. If you wish a copy, the document (ISO 3103:1980) is available for sale for a paltry US$50.[2] Personally, though, I feel that their process is aimed more

---

[2] For more information about ISO 3103:1980, go to TeaWithGary.com and search for the article "The Perfect Cup of Tea part 1."

at making tea for comparative testing than making tea for personal enjoyment. Here is the process that I'd recommend:

1. Start with a high-quality loose-leaf Earl Grey tea.

2. Bring the water to a boil in your tea kettle. Swirl some of the boiling water in your cup and your teapot to heat them up, and then dump out that water.

3. While the kettle returns to a boil, place your dry tea leaves in the teapot. If you're in the United States, use about a tablespoon of leaf for each pint of water. If you're in a country with sensible units of measure, add about 20 grams of leaf for each liter of water.

4. Fill the teapot from the kettle. British wisdom says to always take the teapot to the kettle, for if you take the kettle off of the stove and carry it across the room, the water will be cooling as you walk!

5. If you're drinking it English style, steep for about five minutes, add a dash of milk to the cup, and then pour in the tea. Add sugar to taste.

6. If you're drinking it American style, steep for about three minutes and pour into the cup without adding milk. A good Earl Grey shouldn't require sugar, but feel free to add a lump or two if you prefer it that way.

Once you've tried a cup prepared this way, feel free to experiment. The longer you steep the tea, the more astringent (what Lipton calls "briskness" and everyone else calls "bitterness") it will get. Milk helps to cut the astringency, which is why you steep longer when adding milk.

If the tea needs more body, add more leaf to the teapot. If it doesn't taste strong enough, steep it longer. If it's too strong or has too much bite, you can either sweeten it a bit or use a shorter steeping time.

A lovely variant on traditional Earl Grey tea is the London Fog. It's simply a tea latte, quite easy to make. Instead of using boiling water, brew your Earl Grey tea leaves in a 50-50 mix of boiling water and hot milk. It tastes best when frothed, which you can do with a whisk (as we discussed after the matcha story) or with an electric frother.

The most popular London Fog in my tea bar is what we refer to as an Edinburgh Fog. It's the same drink, but it's made with a lavender Earl Grey. Quite tasty!

Teatime in Georgia
The Birth of Southern Sweet Tea
United States, 1874

One oft-repeated story is that iced tea was invented in 1904 by a vendor named Richard Blechynden at the St. Louis World's Fair. He was having little luck selling hot tea, says the story, and dropped ice cubes in it, thus inventing iced tea. Nice story, but it doesn't account for the 1879 cookbook "Housekeeping in Old Virginia," which includes a recipe for iced Southern sweet tea.

Where did iced tea really come from? Nobody is entirely certain, but it just might have happened like this…

Harriet Suggett adjusted her dress and settled with a sigh into one of the rocking chairs on her veranda. Her husband nodded at her from the other chair and took another draw from the cigar that was clamped between his teeth. Harriet laid the book she was carrying in her lap and sighed again, but louder this time.

"Am I to assume that something is troubling you, dearest?" He took the cigar from his mouth, tapped the ash into the planter that sat between their rockers, and looked at her with a slight smile.

She pointedly ignored the cigar ash in her bougainvillea and pulled her eyebrows into a frown. "Troubling me? Why of *course* something is troubling me, Arthur. That social next Saturday is troubling me!"

"You've had the guest list worked out for a month and the menu worked out for two weeks, Harriet." He held the cigar between his thumb and forefinger, looking at the lazy swirl of smoke rising into the still air. "What could be troubling you about it?"

She eyed him as she would a small child. "What do people serve to drink at social events in Atlanta in the summertime, Arthur Suggett?"

He sensed the trap but couldn't see a way to avoid it. "Tea punch, I would assume."

"Very good. And what's in that punch?"

"I don't know, my dear. It is merely my role to drink it and enjoy it."

"Let me read it to you, then." She opened the somewhat tattered book, which Arthur recognized as a cookbook that Harriet's mother had given her. "This is what Mrs. Lettice Bryanon has to say in her book, *The Kentucky Housewife*":

> "Make a pint and a half of very strong tea in the usual manner; strain it, and pour it boiling on one pound and a quarter of loaf sugar. Add half a pint of rich sweet cream, and then stir in gradually a bottle of claret or of champagne."

She lowered the book back to her lap. "Now do you see?"

Arthur lifted the cigar back to his mouth and took a draw. It was a clear stalling technique that Harriet saw right through. She hadn't spent close to two decades married to the man without learning his tactics. She waited patiently for him to figure it out.

"Is it the wine?" he asked tentatively. "Do we not have enough claret? I can fetch us more quickly enough."

"Oh, you are as thick as a brick, Arthur. Of course it is the wine! We've invited Mrs. Madison!"

Suddenly, it dawned on him. "Emily Madison? Isn't she the one that's starting an Atlanta chapter of that new temperance group for ladies?"

"Yes! The Woman's Christian Temperance Union. It was only last year that it started up in Ohio, and already it's spreading all over. Mrs. Madison is already recruiting here."

"So some of the other ladies are members as well?"

"For goodness' sake, it's not just the ladies. Mr. Wheeler and Reverend Addison are both members of the American Temperance Society, and their wives are as well."

Arthur furrowed his brow and blew a smoke ring. He watched it rise through the still air. "You can't simply leave out the wine, I suppose?"

"Don't you think I've tried that? It tastes simply *horrid* without the wine!"

"And we can't just serve tea?"

"It's *July*, dear Arthur, and we don't have a pavilion. The shade trees burned when the house did, and those little saplings you planted won't be giving us much shade for years yet. Do you really want to drink something hot in the mid-day sun?"

Arthur thought about it. Harriet was right, of course. Since the Yankees burned Atlanta, it had taken almost all of his resources just to rebuild the house. Pavilions and gazebos weren't a possibility for next weekend, and the veranda was far too small for the number of guests they had invited.

They sat silently as they pondered the problem. For twenty long minutes, the only sounds were the creak of the rocking chairs and the exuberant song of a nearby lark. Then Harriet smiled.

"Arthur, can you talk to the ice man and have him triple our delivery next week?"

"Of course, my dear."

"I shall be right back."

She wasn't right back, but that was okay with Arthur. It was a beautiful Sunday afternoon, although rather hotter than he would have preferred. And no matter how the temperance movement developed in Atlanta, he still had his Kentucky bourbon whiskey in the house.

Arthur went in and got himself a glass. He poured the bourbon and looked into the kitchen, where he could see his wife chipping away at a block of ice from the icebox as a kettle whistled on the woodstove behind her. He restrained his curiosity and headed outside with the whiskey glass and a fresh cigar.

When Harriet finally joined him on the veranda, the cigar was half gone and little remained in the bourbon glass. With a smile, she handed him a tall glass of amber liquid with a chunk of ice floating in it. Beads of condensation ran down the side of the glass as he lifted it to study its contents.

"Just taste it," she prodded.

Arthur gave it a tentative taste, cocked his head at her, and then drank deeply.

"What is this?" he asked.

"Tea," she responded with a wide grin. "Strong tea, sugar, and ice. I still need to play with it, but I think I've solved our problem!" She reached for the glass, and Arthur pulled it away and drank it down.

"I think you have."

Harriet worked on her recipe for the next few weeks. Iced tea may seem like a simple concept to you and me, having grown up with it and all, but things were different back then.

Housekeeping in Old Virginia, an 1879 cookbook by Marion Cabell Tyree, suggested that if you want iced tea with dinner, you should steep your green tea leaves in boiling water at breakfast time and allow them to remain in the teapot all day long. The combination of green tea in boiling water and such a long steeping time made for very bitter tea.

In tea punch, that bitterness was offset by sweet cream and a *lot* of sugar. The recipe Harriet was reading from called for 2½ cups of sugar in 3 cups of tea. Without the addition of the dry white wines most Americans drank at the time, the tea punch certainly wouldn't be a tasty drink.

It could not have been a better day for a garden party. A smattering of cottony white clouds provided intermittent relief from the sun, the Atlanta heat was interrupted periodically by cool breezes, and all of the right people were there.

"You and Arthur have done such a wonderful job of rebuilding, Harriet," exclaimed Mrs. Madison.

"Why thank you, Emily!" Harriet sipped her drink, the ice cubes tinkling gently against the glass. "If Arthur hadn't had the foresight to move most of our valuables into the old root cellar by the creek, we'd have lost everything. Absolutely everything."

Emily leaned in conspiratorially, until the brims of their hats nearly touched. Harriet raised an eyebrow.

"It isn't your beautiful home that has us all a-twitter, Harriet."

Harriet gave a half-smile without responding.

"We are all wondering what this wonderful beverage is that you're serving us today. The Reverend Addison said it tasted so good it must be positively sinful, but I told him there was simply no way you'd be serving us any of the demon liquor with all of the temperance people here…" She let the sentence hang.

"Do you want my secret, Emily?"

"Why of course I do!"

"It's just tea, sugar, and ice. It has to be made up the day before, but it really isn't all that complicated."

"You're just a genius, Harriet."

"I am," she smiled.

Preparing sweet tea

About 25 years after Harriet's experiments, Americans started slowly shifting from green tea to black tea, and recipes began to change accordingly. The change shifted into high gear around World War II, when Americans disapproved of almost anything Japanese and switched to Indian (or Ceylon) black teas instead. The basic formula, however, stayed the same.

Here's a tip for my fellow Yankees: if a Southern friend asks for a cup of sweet tea, do not hand them a glass of iced tea and a couple of packets of sweetener. "Sweet tea" and "sweetened tea" are simply not the same thing.

They take their sweet tea quite seriously in Georgia. In 2003, Georgia State Representative John Noel (D-Atlanta), along with four co-sponsors, introduced House Bill 819. The bill demanded that if a restaurant in Georgia served iced tea at all, it must serve sweet tea. The sponsors admitted that the bill was an April Fools Day joke, but that they were half-serious about it. The bill said:

> *(a) As used in this Code section, the term 'sweet tea' means iced tea which is sweetened with sugar at the time that it is brewed.*
>
> *(b) Any food service establishment which served iced tea must serve sweet tea. Such an establishment may serve unsweetened tea but in such case must also serve sweet tea.*
>
> *(c) Any person who violates this Code section shall be guilty of a misdemeanor of a high and aggravated nature.*

There is no universal perfect glass of sweet tea any more than there's a universal perfect cup of tea. There are, however, some simple rules you can follow to keep from embarrassing yourself in front of any guests you may have from Georgia.

Rule 1: Start with strong black tea. Even though sweet tea began as a green tea drink, modern sweet tea is made with black tea steeped longer than most tea aficionados would approve.

Rule 2: Use plain white sugar, and lots of it. No artificial sweetener, no brown sugar, just good old-fashioned cane sugar.

Rule 3: The sugar goes in while the water is hot — preferably while the tea is brewing. Do not add the sugar after you chill the tea!

Rule 4: The tea needs to sit for a while in the fridge before serving. Overnight is good, but plan a few hours at least.

Rule 5: Additional ingredients like lemon and fresh mint leaves are a nice touch, but they are optional. Do not add mint or lemon without asking first. Serve it on the side.

As any black tea drinker knows, the longer you let the tea steep, the stronger and more astringent it gets. For the most part, if you're going to steep that tea longer than five minutes, you'll be adding something to cut the bitterness. Personally, three minutes is plenty for me with most black teas. But with a Southern sweet tea, five minutes is a bare minimum. I've seen recipes calling for anything from seven minutes up to half an hour of steeping time.

Since the tea will be diluted with ice later, it's traditional to use more tea leaf as well. Where I'd use a tablespoon of black tea leaves per pint of water for plain hot black tea, I use twice that much for sweet tea. An ounce of leaf per quart of water is not excessive. Many Southerners make their sweet tea using tea bags, but I think you get better results with loose whole leaf tea.

As per rule 2 above, don't skimp on the sugar, either. About 3/8 of a cup of sugar per quart of water works well, but I know very few Southern belles that would complain if you went up to 1/2 cup. For optimal results, dissolve the sugar completely in the water before steeping the tea in it, and make sure that water is *boiling*.

Once you've removed the tea leaves, put the pitcher in the fridge and let it chill down. For best results, it should be cold before you pour it over the ice to serve it – otherwise the melting ice will dilute the tea too quickly and too much.

I always serve my sweet tea in a tall glass with a straw, and I use clear glass – or plastic if we're around the pool – so that the color of the tea shows.

Sometimes, though, you want a glass of sweet tea, and you want it *right now*.

I am familiar with this syndrome.

If my tea bar was in Georgia, sweet tea wouldn't be a problem for me. I would always have a pitcher or two sitting in the fridge. But here in Montana, the demand for sweet tea is pretty low. If I serve three or four glasses of sweet tea in a week, that's a lot. Why is that a problem? Because, as mentioned above, properly-prepared sweet tea is made in advance. It will keep for a little while, but not indefinitely. If I make it by the pitcher, I'm going to end up throwing most of it away, especially in the winter.

I want to serve sweet tea in my tea bar, and that set my goals for me: it has to taste like sweet tea (in the opinion of my Southern friends), and I have to be able to prepare it from scratch in about five minutes.

I fiddled with solutions to the problem for quite some time, and I think I've come up with an acceptable solution. My method is based on my 20-ounce iced tea glasses, my ice machine (which makes very small cubes), and various other things specific to my own shop. Obviously, you'll need to tweak it a bit for your own use.

For sweetening iced teas (especially boba tea), I keep simple syrup on hand all of the time. We make it using equal quantities of boiling water and plain sugar, and then cool it down to room temperature. It's much easier than trying to mix granulated sugar into cold tea.

First, I put a tablespoon of strong black tea leaves in the infuser — I use a strong Irish Breakfast Tea with finely broken ("CTC") leaves, which maximizes the surface area for steeping.

To the leaves, I add four tablespoons of simple syrup and about 10oz of boiling water. I suppose I could use artificial sweeteners, but I have never heard a request for diet sweet tea. If it's not real sweet tea with sugar, it's just sweetened tea, I suppose.

While it is steeping, I fill the glass all the way to the brim with ice.

I steep the tea for five minutes. I would never steep a cup of Irish breakfast tea that long for myself — especially with that much leaf — because I'm a bit of a purist and I don't add milk or sugar. Steeping that long makes plain tea very bitter. Using this much sugar, however, offsets that bitterness, and adding it during the steep makes the tea taste different than if it's added after the fact.

When the tea is poured over the ice, most of the ice will melt. Add a straw and you're good to go.

Oriental Beauty
The Braggart's Tea
Taiwan, 1931

Huang was very good at keeping his head down. He came from a prominent Hakka family that had been farming in Beipu for many generations, but since his father and brother were killed almost 25 years ago, Huang tried not to draw too much attention to himself.

The aftermath of the Beipu uprising had been difficult for him and his mother. When the locals attacked some of the Japanese officials that controlled this part of occupied Taiwan, retaliation was swift and harsh. Huang was only twelve years old at the time, but he understood more than his parents gave him credit for. His father and older brother, Chou, talked a lot – too much, as it turns out – about how much they resented and hated the outsiders that had taken over their country. It made them heroes among the local Hakka people, but made them targets for the Japanese.

After the dust settled, Huang and his mother never could have kept their small tea farm going without the help of their neighbors. He grew into a man that the locals liked and the Japanese officials didn't notice.

And that leads us to the summer of 1931.

Huang faced an insidious enemy that seemed just too numerous to fight. Not the Japanese; they mostly left him alone. The tea green leafhoppers. These tiny insects did a disproportionately huge amount of damage to the tea crops around Beipu. Unfortunately, they didn't just attack the stems, but went after the leaves and the tender valuable buds as well. They were a problem every year, but this year it was awful.

"Come, Mother," he said one morning, much more subdued than usual. "Let us see if we have a crop to harvest."

His mother Lin looked him over. She saw much of her husband in his features, but the attitude and confidence seemed gone today. She stood up gingerly. She was getting close to 60 years old, but so were a lot of the other tea pickers in her area. Though her joints may have ached, she was still strong and proud. She went outside with Huang.

The two of them walked down the rows of carefully-tended bushes, and Huang felt like crying as he surveyed the damage.

"We have so little," he said. "Why must we lose the only thing that can feed us this winter?"

"The ways of the bodhisattvas are beyond our knowing," Lin answered, referring to the Buddhist gods. "We must take what they give us and figure out how to make it work."

"But we can't harvest this! The whole crop is ruined, just like our neighbors' crops. There are more leafhoppers on these plants than buds. There isn't an un-chewed leaf in sight. Everybody on this side of Beipu is just giving up on tea this year."

"When things got bad, did your father give up? Did your brother give up?"

"No. And look where it got them! They're dead!"

Lin gave Huang a withering look, and turned her back on him. She stood for a moment, tears running down her face, and then began to walk away.

"Wait, Mother! I didn't mean to…"

He started to move toward her and then just stopped and stood. He watched her until she'd gone into the house and closed the door behind her, and then he dropped his gaze to his feet. A gentle breeze wafted by and a leafhopper jumped from the closest plant onto his face. Huang closed his eyes, ignoring the insect. For several minutes, he stood there, shoulders slumped and head down, the leafhopper perched on his forehead. And then he made a decision.

Huang's eyes opened, and fire blazed in them. His back straightened, his head came up, and he surveyed the field. In one swift motion, he grabbed the leafhopper on his face, crushed it between his fingers, and flung it to the ground. Without looking at it, he strode purposefully to the house, mind racing, stirring up a cloud of leafhoppers as his sleeves brushed the tea bushes to both sides of him.

When he opened the door, Lin didn't look up. She sat at the table with a cup of tea, her back to the door.

"You're right, Mother. Father wouldn't have given up. Chou wouldn't have given up, either. No matter how bad things got, they always found a way to make it work, and now it is my turn.

"We will pick this crop, we will process it, and I will take it to the market! I may sell it to the Taiwanese tea masters, and I may sell to the foreigners, but I will sell it, and you won't believe how much I will get from them!"

She stood and turned to face him. For a moment, they just looked at each other. She was calm, expressionless. He stood ramrod-straight, breathing heavily. She reached out and took his face in her hands.

"You *are* like your father; you talk too much. He would say that we need three things to make the tea: heaven, earth, and ourselves. Heaven has provided us with good weather, and our soil is good. Now it is our turn. Go. Get everything ready. I will get some girls to help us pick the tea."

Huang looked at his mother and the women from the neighboring farms. If this was to work, it would have to be done just right.

"You all know how to pick tea," he began. Heads nodded and one woman laughed. "But this year is different. Look carefully at this plant."

He pinched and twisted slightly to remove a small branch, about eight inches long, and held it up, casually brushing several leafhoppers from it. He motioned at the larger leaves near the base of the stem.

"We won't pick the larger leaves at all," he told them. "The damage is too extensive this year, so if I'm to produce a usable crop, it shall have to be from the buds and the two smallest leaves."

The women nodded. They'd been fighting the leafhoppers for a long time; many years they had left half of their crop un-harvested. They weren't sure what Huang had in mind, though, so they listened carefully.

"Even if the leaves have been chewed, I want you to pick them. Take the bud and two leaves together, and collect all you can – even those with spots or white tips on the buds. We're harvesting late this year, so we don't have very much time."

"It won't be much of a crop if we pick the white tips and spotty leaves," one of the women said. Lin glared at her and she cringed slightly.

"I have a plan," Huang responded, full of false bravado. "This is going to be the most amazing batch of tea we've ever produced. Just watch! Now, thank you for helping us, and let's get going."

The tea pickers slung their baskets on their hips and set to work. It was a small field and an experienced group of pickers, and since they were ignoring the larger leaves, the picking went quite fast. At the end of the day, when the tea pickers had gone, Huang and his mother surveyed the depressingly small piles of leaves and buds, with little brown spots where the plant had tried to heal itself.

"Father would have called this an opportunity," Huang said. Lin looked at him dubiously.

"Most of the farmers here have abandoned their crops this year," he continued, "so there is a shortage of tea. Maybe that means that I will be in a better position to negotiate at market."

"Stop dreaming and get to work," she replied, but she hid a smile as she walked away.

Huang had no idea what the hoppers had done to the leaves. He looked at the white tips and brown spots only as damage. In a normal year, he would have thrown away most of what was spread out before him this year. What he didn't know is that there were several factors at play that would work in his favor.

First, the insect bites had exposed parts of the leaves to the air and started a slow oxidation while the leaves were still on the plant. Second, the plants had begun to produce chemical compounds to heal the damage. This combination would have a drastic effect on the tea.

When they finished loading up the cases of completed tea for market, Huang took his mother's arm and led her over to a small table in the drying and rolling shed. On the table was a bowl of tea leaves.

"I picked the best I could find from this harvest," he told her, as they looked over the bowl. It did, in fact, look pretty much like every other harvest they'd ever had. "This is what I'll serve the buyers who wish to taste."

"You can't do that. They'll be angry if the tea they sample isn't the same as what they buy."

He sighed. "You're right, of course."

"Come," she said. "Let's grab a handful of leaves at random and see what we've created."

They opened up a chest and pulled out enough leaves for a pot of tea.

"I already have water heating in the house," Lin told him as they walked through their tiny vegetable garden.

"It is a bit more oxidized than usual," he said. "Let's keep the steep time fairly short."

She tossed some leaves into a teapot, gauging the amount of tea with a practiced eye. She added the water, a bit cooler than usual, as Huang fetched two cups. After a few moments, Lin poured the tea for them.

"The color is nice," Huang said hopefully. Indeed, the tea was a beautiful dark orange against the stark white of the teacups. He lifted the cup to his nose, and his eyes widened.

"Mother! Smell it!" She lifted her cup as well.

"It smells like honey," she said, pausing to breathe deeply. "And peaches."

They sipped together and smiled as they looked at each other.

"I think you *will* be able to sell this," she told him.

Huang sauntered into the tea market mid-morning and set up his stall. There were fewer farmers than usual, as most of his neighbors hadn't shown up. Since word of the leafhopper blight had spread, there were also fewer buyers. Huang's confidence began to crack as the Taiwanese tea experts looked over his leaves and moved on, despite his urging to taste the tea. The Japanese generally scorned the Taiwan oolongs, preferring their steamed green teas, so Huang worried that he wouldn't even get a nibble.

It was early afternoon before one of the English buyers strolled down his aisle. The English tended to travel more, and were more open to experimenting with new varietals and new processes. This could be his chance!

Huang greeted the Englishman enthusiastically, and offered him a taste of the tea.

"What am I tasting?" asked the buyer in pidgin Chinese.

"Something new this year," Huang replied. "Taste, please, and then I shall show you the leaves."

The English buyer sniffed cautiously and slurped loudly at the tea. Huang repressed a shudder at what he considered coarse manners.

"This is intriguing. It is oolong, obviously, but quite unique. Sweeter. Lovely, actually."

Huang laid the wet leaves from the pot out on one small plate and slid another plate out next to it with dry leaves.

"What are these white tips?"

"That's my secret," Huang said. "I'll bet you've never seen anything like it, have you?"

"How much do you want for it?" the Englishman asked warily.

Huang made a quick appraisal of the buyer, took a deep breath, and quoted well over triple what he normally charged. There was a long pause, and they stared at each other without blinking.

I've got him, Huang thought. If he wasn't interested, he would have just walked away, but he's standing here trying to decide what to counter-offer!

The buyer countered with the usual market rate for Beipu oolongs. The negotiation proceeded as negotiations tend to proceed. Eventually, the Englishman offered twice Huang's usual price.

"I can do that," Huang responded slowly, "but only if you take all of it. At this price, I don't want to spend the rest of the day here dickering with other buyers."

"Done and done."

The transaction was soon finalized, and Huang headed home, radiating excitement. Even with less tea than he'd taken to market last year, he was far ahead monetarily, and the swagger was back in his step. When he got to the house, Lin was out in the yard with several of the neighbors. He nearly danced over to them.

"I don't suppose I need to ask how it went," she said with a smile.

"It's amazing, Mother! I'm so glad we saved a bag for ourselves. The local buyers weren't interested, but I sold all of the rest to an Englishman for *double* the normal price!"

"Double? You must be joking," said the man who owned the farm just south of theirs.

"Yes," said his wife. "You're just bragging."

"Oh, no no," Huang responded. "You must try this. It is the most amazing tea we've ever made. We've been so silly throwing away the white-tipped buds and the chewed leaves."

"Here," said Lin, "I'll go inside and make a pot of our new tea for everyone to try."

"Are you saying that this hopper-chewed mess actually makes good tea?" the first neighbor asked, waving his arm at the tea field.

"No, I'm not saying it makes good tea. I'm saying it makes *great* tea!"

"And I'm still saying you're a braggart," the wife said.

Huang laughed. Not a chuckle that escaped in a couple of quick breaths, nor the polite snicker that acknowledges a particularly bad joke. No, this was a great deep belly laugh that took all of the stress of the last few weeks and let it all come pouring out. Most came out as sound, some was squeezed from his eyes in the form of tears.

They were still watching the last cathartic tear wind its way through the road dust on Huang's face when Lin returned with a tray of filled teacups. She held it out to each in turn, and each took a teacup filled with their latest creation. Huang and Lin watched the neighbors' expressions become serious as they smelled and sipped at the tea.

"The gods have smiled upon you, Huang," the neighbor said, bowing deeply. "And you, of course, Lin. And now a new question arises."

"Yes?" responded Huang cautiously.

"Will you be showing your friends how to make your braggart's tea?"

He did, of course, show them what he had done, or we wouldn't have a very nice ending to our story. Braggart's tea ("peng feng cha") grew increasingly popular in Beipu and the rest of Hsinchu county, eventually spreading to other parts of Taiwan.

When an English tea trader presented some to Queen Victoria, she promptly dubbed it Oriental Beauty ("dongfang meiren"), the name it is best known by today, although many tea shops prefer the names "White Tip Oolong" or "Bai Hao."

About Oriental Beauty

As the story tells us, Oriental Beauty is a fairly low-yield crop. Even today, growers use no pesticides because the effect of the leafhoppers' bites is an integral part of the tea. On top of that, it uses only the bud and adjoining two leaves from the tea plant, lowering the amount of tea produced by an acre of bushes even more.

All of this adds up to an expensive tea. You can expect Oriental Beauty to cost at least double what the average oolong costs, although it is far from being the priciest oolong tea. It is, however, well worth trying.

When you shop for Oriental Beauty, make sure you keep in mind all of its other names. The exact same tea may be offered in four shops with four different names. Although some are more common than others, I've seen bai hao, dongfang meiren, peng feng cha, white tip, braggart's tea, bragger's tea, champagne oolong, and Oriental Beauty on menus and in catalogs.

Oriental Beauty is still produced in Hsinchu County, where Beipu is located, and many connoisseurs insist that Hsinchu's Oriental Beauty is still the best. If you can find some from that area, try it first. But then, broaden your horizons. The leafhoppers are found in a lot of warmer low-altitude parts of Taiwan, and similar tea-munching insects can be found in other countries. I even have some Oriental Beauty tea from northern India.

Unlike some other oolongs, Oriental Beauty leaves are not typically rolled into tight balls. They are twisted, however, and will uncurl in the pot or infuser. Despite its generally high oxidation level (most Oriental Beauty teas are about 70% oxidized), it's best if you do not use boiling water. Instead, use cooler water – about 175°F (80°C).

Use half a tablespoon of leaves for each cup of water, and steep it for a fairly short time. There is no single "right" way to make any tea, but I'd suggest trying a two minute steep the first time, and then steeping longer if you want a stronger infusion.

As with most other oolongs, you can re-use the leaves at least three or four times. Steep about a half minute longer with each successive steeping. Being able to brew four cups of tea from one serving of leaves makes the generally expensive Oriental Beauty much more of a bargain.

Post-Apocalyptic Earl Grey

Australia, 20 years from now

I motion the others down and creep carefully to the top of the hill. Poking my head up as little as possible, I scan the arid land slowly with my binoculars, shading the lenses with my left hand to avoid giving away our presence with reflected sunlight.

Scrub, mostly. A small mob of roos at a tiny billabong about a kilometre away. Aside from the billabong, cover is limited to sparse, scraggly trees that look like they've just about given up on growing. But there! What's that between those hills, right where the old road winds through?

"Well, Sam?" comes Sheila's stage whisper from just behind me.

In no particular hurry, I put the lens covers on the binoculars and slide quietly backward to join the group, taking care not to kick up any dust.

"The *good* news is, there's a town about ten clicks out," I announce. Then I pause, knowing that Sheila is going to finish the thought for me. And so she does:

"And the *bad* news is, there's a town about ten clicks out."

Towns mean a lot of good things. New clothes, ammo, fresh batteries, packaged and dried foods, and sometimes even warm beds in a secure location.

But towns mean danger, too. Creepers. Zombies. The walking dead. Creepers concentrate in towns, probably because that's where they were when they died. I think as their brains deteriorate, they find comfort in familiar surroundings. The bigger the town, the more creepers you'll find there.

"If we head in now, we'll reach it right around dusk," observes Andrew. He's quite the strategist. I make a pretty good leader, and I try to stay three jumps ahead of the circumstances, but Andrew's usually another jump or two ahead of me. "If we don't know the area, that's a pretty bad idea. I suggest we make camp here and hit the town in the morning."

Sheila, Zane, and Angela wearily survey our surroundings. There's not much cover and not much shade – just one lonely tree – although it's not overly hot at the moment. We could probably dig out a halfway comfortable place to sleep. We don't have much food left, but I certainly don't feel like hunting this afternoon, especially with a town that close.

"We'll camp here tonight," I announce. "One more night of cold rations, and then hopefully a bounty when we hit the town tomorrow."

Sheila is crouched down, digging through her pack. "I don't know about the rest of you, but I'm pretty low on ammo for an assault on a town."

"If you'd just use the same weapons we use, we could share our ammo with you," Zane tells her.

He has a point. There's a reason that the rest of us decided on the 9mm Glocks as our pistol of choice. They're lightweight and reliable, ammo is plentiful, and they're easy to handle – even for a tiny sheila like Sheila.

Sheila rolls her eyes at him. "When I shoot one of those ratbags, I want it to go down and stay down." She slams home a full clip and hoists the .44 magnum she carries. "Use your girlie guns if you want, but I'm sticking with this bad boy."

She rises fluidly to her feet and faces him. They make quite a contrast, those two. Sheila is 45 kilos soaking wet, short red hair that looks like it was cut with a chainsaw, and dressed in loose, baggy clothing. Her green eyes are flashing as she looks up into Zane's face.

Zane, on the other hand, is a metre ninety-three of bulging muscles. His 100 kilos are packed into a t-shirt that's about ready to rip at the seams and a pair of shorts with more pockets than a wallaby ranch. His jet-black hair flows halfway down his back, and he shoots Sheila a smile that's all teeth and sparkling eyes.

"If I drop a creeper at 30 metres with my 'girlie guns,' it won't be getting back up, luv."

"Oh, get a room, you two," Angela cuts in. "Come on, Andrew, let's make camp."

As Andrew and Angela start unpacking, I turn to Zane and Sheila.

"I'll head over to the billabong and get us some water. You two get some food ready."

"I'm coming with you," Zane says.

"Ah, it's only a click out and —"

"— and your rules say that nobody leaves camp alone. Not even to hit the dunny."

I sigh. He's right, of course. Even bathroom breaks are done in pairs.

"Fine. Sheila, you take care of tucker while Z-man and I get the water."

She gives me a withering look. "Let the girl handle the kitchen while you do the fun stuff, eh?"

She's not really mad. I know it, and she knows I know it. After a quick glare – just enough for show – she sets to work pulling out pouches of prepared foods along with a few fruits and veggies we've gathered in the last couple of days.

The water expedition is uneventful, and we're back in camp in nothing flat with all of the canteens full and an extra water sack for washing up. Everyone finds a place to park under the tree, and Sheila passes around the tucker as Zane hands out the water.

"What I'd give for a proper beer with dinner," Angela says.

Zane smiles. "Or two. Or three. Or four…"

"If we're lucky, this town hasn't already been looted and we can find ourselves a few cases of stubbies tomorrow," Sheila kicks in.

"That would be luck, indeed," Angela smiles.

"I don't know about the rest of you mugs," I add, "but I haven't had a decent cup of tea since this damned breakout started. I love a good beer as much as the next bloke, but the tea's a lot better with brekkie."

"Well, it's not brekkie now, Sam," Angela says, "It's dinner. As good as tea would be in the morning, I'd rather have a beer tonight."

"Fair enough, Angela. Fair enough."

We tuck into dinner – such as it is – as the sun sets. By the time we finish and clean up, it's getting pretty dark.

"Let's get some sleep," Andrew says. "I think we'll be hitting the road pretty early tomorrow."

We're all up with the sun, and take care of our morning ablutions and eliminations in no time. After six months wandering through the outback, we're pretty quick at breaking camp. Everyone's eager to hit the town, and sick of raw veggies, so we decide to skip breakfast and head straight out.

We creep to the top of the hill and I point out where the road cuts through the little pass to the town. I direct the team down the hill, parallel to the road. Zane takes point, Andrew and the sheilas go in the middle, and I bring up the rear.

"You know what I want tonight?" Andrew doesn't wait for a response. "I want to sleep in a proper bed with a real pillow instead of sleeping on this bedroll in the dirt like a swagman."

"I still want beer," Angela adds. "And maybe a bath."

The banter continues until we reach the foot of the hill north of the town, when I shush everyone. The creepers aren't organized enough or smart enough to post guards, but that doesn't mean we won't find one wandering around outside of town.

We move into a tighter formation and move up to an outcropping of rock right at the top of the hill.

"Take a peek, Andrew. How's it look?" His bushcraft isn't as good as the rest of us, but it's always good to have the tactician scope out the situation. He works his way up the rocks and peeks carefully over the top. After a moment, Sheila starts to say something and I stop her. You just need to let Andrew take his time.

When he finally comes back down, he has a smile on his face.

"The town's pretty small, but —" he starts, and Sheila groans. "*But*, we have a clear approach with good cover. I see some creepers, but not that many, and mostly at the other end of town. And guess what's at this end of town?"

Everyone looks at him.

"A hotel with a *pub!* If they haven't trashed the place, we'll have locking doors, beds, and booze tonight!"

"What about supplies?" Zane asks.

"I was getting there. Looks like there's a restaurant of some kind across from the hotel. I can't see the front from this angle, so I'm not sure what. And there's a store a block down that may have the rest of what we need."

"So let's do it," Sheila says, pulling out her .44 and racking the slide.

"Hang tight a sec." It seems like I'm always trying to hold her back. "I want to move in quietly and take out any creepers we find without your hand cannon alerting every creeper in town. Angela, get your bow ready."

You want Angela at your back when the zombies show up. She's not an "up close and personal" fighter like Zane, but she's deadly accurate with any kind of ranged weapon. She can put an arrow in a moving creeper's eye from a block away, and she's saved my arse more than once with throwing knives and a particularly wicked hatchet that she favors.

I hear the whisper of Zane's sword leaving its scabbard. That sword makes me nervous. We're still not sure how the creeper disease spreads. Zane thinks it's only from bites. I think it could be any bodily fluid transfer – like getting creeper blood splattered all over you when you behead one with a sword. But on the other hand, if the creepers get close enough to be a danger, Zane is quick and quiet, so I don't say anything.

"Don't use the guns unless you have to, and stay close together. We'll go straight to the hotel and take control of the pub, and then strategize from there. If there's any problem with getting into the hotel, plan B is the restaurant Andrew spotted. Got it?"

All four of them nod. I pull the Glocks out of the shoulder holster, chamber a round, flip on the safety, and put it back. Then I do the same with the one on my hip. I heard the sounds of everyone else doing the same. Sheila, of course, kept that monstrous .44 out and ready to go. Clint Eastwood would be proud.

We move out.

Half a year of operating as a team makes this a lot easier. We sweep down the hillside to the road, where a lone creeper wanders aimlessly. Angela drops it with a single arrow, which she recovers, wipes on what's left of the creeper's clothes, and loosely re-nocks.

We can now clearly see the hotel, which looks to be in good shape. Across the street, most of the buildings are burned out, but the restaurant sits in the middle of its lot, untouched by the fires. Some of the damage is recent. There's still smoke rising from the crumbled ruins of one of the buildings.

We keep moving.

There's another creeper on the front steps of the hotel, and she takes it out using the same arrow. I step over the body and carefully open the front door. Damn. I knew this was too easy.

Everything becomes a blur. Two zombies, fresh enough to still be able to move quickly, come at me from inside the hotel. I jump backward, trip over the body on the stairs, and end up flat on my back, knocking down Angela as I go. Sheila's gun roars, turning the first one's head into a cloud of pink mist. My Glock clears the holster just as Zane steps in and takes the head off of the second one.

The sound of Sheila's gun draws the attention of every creeper in the area. Angela and I get to our feet, weapons drawn, as we hear more commotion inside the hotel and see several zombies heading our way on the street. Zane slams the lobby door and kicks the body of the creeper he just killed against it. An arrow whizzes past me into one of the creepers on the street as Andrew and Sheila open fire on the other two.

"Restaurant," I yell, as I head across the street.

When I reach the door, I see that the restaurant is actually a tea house. Cool! When this is over, there had better be some tea in there!

I swing around to put my back against the wall and make sure the rest of my group is heading my way. The creepers in the street are down, but there are a couple more coming behind them about two blocks away. Another has just pushed the hotel door open. I aim carefully and put two slugs in that one as everyone else reaches the tea house.

The routine is well-rehearsed. Sheila and Angela look through the windows. When they call out the all-clear, Zane goes through the door with Andrew right behind him. I scan the street, taking a shot at another creeper by the corner of the building.

Zane's shout of "clear" from inside the tea house seems louder than Sheila's gun. Everyone swings into the tea house, and we lock the door. There's a side room that's not visible from the front windows, and we all move into there except for Sheila, who ducked behind the counter.

The place looks untouched.

"That door was unlocked," Andrew says with a puzzled expression on his face. "Why haven't they been in here?"

I have no idea. There's a layer of dust on everything, and a bit of ash from the fires, but not a single cup is broken, nor a single chair knocked over.

"Obviously, the outbreak hit this town when the restaurant was closed," he continues, "so nobody was inside when they got infected."

"Either that or they just ran straight home when they heard it on the radio," Sheila chimes in. "That would explain the unlocked door, and the cash in the till. Hell, there's still some full cups of tea on a tray back here, along with some nasty dried-up scones."

"*All* scones are nasty and dried up," Zane says. I don't bother to answer. Zane's an American. What does he know?

"Shhh. Down." Sheila motions us away from the main room. She peeks over the counter, looking toward the front door with gun at the ready. After a long moment, she stands up.

"There is something seriously strange going on here. That creeper walked up to the door, looked in, and then left. I'm sure it saw me, but it just left."

We walked out into the room. No creepers were visible outside the windows except for the ones we had killed and the one Sheila saw, which was shambling away from us.

"Okay, let's settle in here for a bit and figure out what we're doing. Zane and Sheila, check the front and side room. Angela and Andrew, check the rest of the building. I'm going to start a little fire and heat up some water for tea."

I coax a flame out of the collection of old paper cups and napkins in the wastebasket, and then dump it in the sink. I bust the back off of one of the delicate wooden chairs and add the wood from the chairs to the fire. Once it's going, I crisscross a few knives over the sink to make a platform for a tea kettle. I find a kettle and fill it up with water. As I prop it on precarious platform of knives over the flames. Andrew comes in through the kitchen door.

"I don't think I've ever seen that much tea in one place in my life, Sam!"

I follow him through the door. Holy cow! Dozens of big Tupperware containers, each probably holding five kilos of black loose-leaf tea. More tea is spread out in big metal trays, and a spray bottle is sitting between two of the trays. I sniff at the tea. It has absorbed a lot of the smoke from the fires in this block, but it's pretty clear what it is. Earl Grey!

I check out the spray bottle. Yep. It's bergamot oil. This place obviously made its own Earl Grey tea, and was just in the middle of spraying a batch when the zombie infestation swept through town. The tea has been sitting out on the trays for months, so it's pretty dried out, but I'm holding a sprayer of bergamot. I tentatively spritz the leaves in the closest tray a few times to moisten them and refresh that Earl Grey smell, and then I hear a gasp from behind me.

I turn to see Andrew, wide-eyed, pulling out his 9mm. Following his gaze, I see that the back door is standing open and there are two creepers at the screen. They lock eyes with me and I hold up my hand in front of Andrew to stop him from shooting. The creepers back away from the door and wander away.

"What the bloody hell was that about, Sam? They just left! They stood and looked at you, and just *left*!"

"I don't know, Andrew. This whole thing is weird. Why won't they come in here?"

We walk into the other room to talk to the others just as the kettle begins to whistle. I put some of the tea leaves I just sprayed into a teapot and add the boiling water. Oh, that smell is wonderful! It's smoky from the fire, but the Earl Grey aroma kicks through extra strong from that last spritz of bergamot oil I just added to it.

"Bergamot oil!" Everyone turns to look at me. "That's it! It's the bergamot oil!"

I run back to the blending room, grab the sprayer, and begin spritzing my clothes. Then I draw my gun and head for the door.

"What the hell do you think you're doing, Sam?" Angela yells.

Gun in one hand and sprayer in the other, I charge through the screen. Three creepers are pawing through the rubble from the burned out building behind the tea house, and they rise and head toward me. I keep coming, my companions yelling at me to stop.

As I get close, the creepers stop. I slow to a walk and continue toward them. Confused, they start backing away. I charge at one and spray bergamot oil in its face. The creeper *screams*. Creepers make a lot of different noises. They grunt, they growl, they gurgle. But one thing I have never heard from a creeper is a full-on scream.

The rest of my group skids to a halt behind me, bristling with weapons. The creeper I sprayed is pawing at its face and continuing to scream as the others hustle away in opposite directions. I stand there watching until the roar of Sheila's .44 right by my ear almost deafens me. The creeper crumbles to the ground.

"It's the bergamot oil."

I don't know how long this stash of bergamot will last us, but since a good spritzing on our clothes will keep the creepers at bay for weeks, I imagine these six huge jugs of it are good for a very long time.

We've completely cleared the town now, and set up defensible living quarters in the hotel. There's food and supplies enough to last us a year or more, and more tea than I can possibly drink. We've got a generator working, and Angela's trying to build a radio transmitter so we can spread the word about our miracle oil.

I've nicknamed the smoky blend from the trays "post-apocalyptic Earl Grey," and I'm quite enjoying it.

Welcome back, civilization. I've missed you.

About Post-Apocalyptic Earl Grey

This story may be set 20 years in the future, but the tea it's based on exists now. The real story behind the tea is, perhaps, as intriguing as the legend. It all began when Twining's changed their formulation for Earl Grey back in 2011. The tea world was all a-twitter about the change – or at least the Earl Grey lovers were – and I started a discussion on my favorite message board about it. Here's where things got interesting.

During the discussion, a fellow who uses the online moniker "Mr. Excellent" commented:

> *"But yah, Twinings is acceptable, but I prefer to get my tea from a local tea shop. And lapsang souchong is more my thing, anyway. (Though adding bergamot could be neat...)"*

The idea of a smoky lapsang souchong with bergamot just seemed wonderful to me, and I commented that I was going to give a shot at creating one. Mr. Excellent responded with:

Over the course of the day, I played with recipes, and drank a lot
of tea. By mid-afternoon, I was getting fairly close to what I
wanted, and described it thus:

My goal was to create a blend that would make you feel like you
were sitting among the smoldering remains of civilization, enjoying
a nice cup of tea before hefting your shotgun and going back to
fighting off the zombies. After another week or so of
experimentation, I decided that I'd hit it. "Mr. Excellent's Post-
Apocalyptic Earl Grey" went on the menu at the tea bar, and it's
been one of our top Earl Grey teas ever since.

Glossary

Beipu Uprising: A 1907 armed Hakku uprising against the Japanese occupation of Taiwan, which began in 1895.

Bergamot: A citrus fruit related to the orange. Most of the world's bergamot production comes from Italy.

Bodhisattva: A Buddhist "god" or "goddess."

Camellia sinensis: The tea plant, which produces all of the teas described in this book.

Chaki: Matcha tea caddy. Also used as a generic term for any matcha tea implement.

Chanoyu: The "way of tea" and basis for the Japanese tea ceremony. Based on the four principles of wa (harmony), kei (respect), sei (purity), and jaku (tranquility).

Chashaku: Matcha scoop.

Chasen: Matcha whisk.

Chawan: Matcha bowl.

Earl Grey: A tea (usually black tea) with oil of bergamot added to it. Named for Charles, the 2nd Earl Grey.

Fixing: The stage of tea processing where the leaves are steamed, baked, or pan-fried to stop (or prevent) oxidation.

Guanyin: The Goddess (bodhisattva) of Mercy.

Hakka: A group of Han Chinese people known for their migratory ways. They originated in China, but have settled all over the world. Over 15% of the population of Taiwan is Hakka.

Koicha: The "thick matcha" used in a Japanese tea ceremony.

Leafhoppers: The "tea green leafhoppers" described in the Oriental Beauty story in this book are *Jacobiasca formosana*, tiny leaf-sucking insects about a tenth of an inch long.

L-Theanine: An amino acid found in tea that has relaxing properties and also softens the "caffeine crash" found in other caffeinated drinks such as coffee.

Matcha: Japanese powdered green tea.

Pharmacopoeia: A book of medicines with their effects and instructions for use.

Sen no Rikyū (1522-1591): Tea master to daimyo Toyotomi Hideyoshi, Rikyū is credited with creating the Japanese tea ceremony as we know it today.

Shennong (28th century BC): The legendary Chinese emperor also known as the Emperor of the Five Grains. He is credited with creating the first pharmacopoeia and introducing agriculture, acupuncture, and tea to China.

Teaku: A term coined by a group of tea bloggers to refer to haiku about tea.

Tieguanyin: Iron Goddess of Mercy oolong tea. Also spelled tie guanyin, tie guan yin, ti kuan yin, tie kwun yin, tae guan yin, and quite a few other ways.

Usucha: The "thin matcha" usually consumed as an everyday matcha drink.

Wabi-sabi: A philosophy that treasures transience, asymmetry, and imperfection.

Withering: The first stage of processing after tea leaves are picked. Withering removes excess moisture and allows slight oxidation.

About the Author

Gary Robson is a tea blogger and owner of a tea bar in, of all places, a small town in Montana.

He started out in the technology world and became a vocal advocate of closed captioning on television for deaf and hard-of-hearing people. In his endless quest to figure out what he's going to be when he grows up, he has been granted a couple of patents, teamed up with family members to start an electronics business and a software business, run a small newspaper and a bookstore, taught computer science, written 20 books about poop, raised some cattle, done a little standup comedy, put on seminars all over the country, given a TED (well … TEDx) talk, and competed in rodeos.

Luckily for him, Gary's wife and kids are good at smiling tolerantly and putting up with him.

Myths & Legends of Tea, volume 1 is Gary's 25th book.

GaryDRobson.com

TeaWithGary.com

You can also find Tea With Gary on Facebook and Twitter.

Other Books
by Gary D. Robson

Children's Picture Books

The *Who Pooped in the Park?* books teach children about animal scat and tracks in different ecosystems around the United States. Six of the books are illustrated by Elijah Brady Clark, and the rest by Robert Rath.

Who Pooped in the Black Hills?
Who Pooped in the Cascades?
Who Pooped in Central Park? (New York City)
Who Pooped in the Park? (Acadia National Park)
Who Pooped in the Park? (Big Bend National Park)
Who Pooped on the Colorado Plateau?
Who Pooped in the Park? (Death Valley National Park)
Who Pooped in the Park? (Glacier National Park)
Who Pooped in the Park? (Grand Canyon National Park)
Who Pooped in the Park? (Grand Teton National Park)
Who Pooped in the North Woods?
Who Pooped in the Park? (Olympic National Park)
Who Pooped in the Park? (Red Rock Canyon National Conservation Area)
Who Pooped in the Redwoods?
Who Pooped in the Park? (Rocky Mountain National Park)
Who Pooped in the Park? (Sequoia/Kings Canyon National Parks)
Who Pooped in the Park? (Shenandoah National Park)
Who Pooped in the Sonoran Desert?
Who Pooped in the Park? (Yellowstone National Park)
Who Pooped in the Park? (Yosemite National Park)

And don't miss Gary's *A Tea Journey: Your Personal Tea Journal*, a guided journal designed to guide you through the next 100 teas you taste. Keeping notes about each cup of tea encourages you to drink your tea actively, paying attention to taste, aroma, appearance, and how it feels in your mouth. When you journal about it, tea becomes an experience to savor and linger over instead of just another drink.